The Shack

Michael Gabriel

The Shack

by Michael Gabriel

Copyright © 2017 by Michael Gabriel

All rights reserved.

ISBN: 9781549811623

DEDICATION

"Dedicated to those who fell and to those who carry on"

CONTENTS

ACKNOWLEDGMENTS

To my life-coach, my best friend Nicole: because I owe it all to you. Many Thanks!

1. STARTING OVER

The rain beat violently down on my mother's rusty Chevy Citation, as we traveled to Sherbrook, Maine to start our new lives. It had been a continuous downpour since we left Scranton, Pennsylvania at six this morning, and the rain was a depressing reminder of how much I was going to miss my old life. My name is Justin Spencer, and it is June 15, 1988: the day my mother and I decided to run away from our past. Being the stubborn 15-year-old that I am, I protested the move, but Mom ignored my pleas with deaf ears as usual.

How was I supposed to forget the only people I had ever known, and pretend as though the only life I had ever known never existed? On the other hand, I suppose I wasn't going to miss it all that much.

The only friend that I had in Scranton-or anywhere for that matter—was Alex Reilly. Alex was a boy with a mild learning disability who had lived next door to me. We shared a common interest in old horror comics, such as: *Tales from The Crypt*, *Adventures into Terror*, and *Dark Mysteries*. We would spend hours during our Friday night sleepovers, just reading, and discussing these stories that never became tiresome to us.

Horror comics were our escape from the mundane, but that was about the extent of our friendship. Now that I think about it, I was probably going to miss Alex's comic books more than Alex, himself. It's kind of sad really.

I guess I've always been sort of a loner. I could tolerate people in small doses, but after a while, they would pierce my ears and nerves with every annoying mannerism that their bodies could conjure. This had been the world that I lived in, ever since I was old enough to think logically. I would put on a fake smile and carry on conversations with those who wanted me to speak, but on the inside, it was a chore that drained my body of all its energy. After such mental exhaustion, my body would require days of solitude and rest to fully recover. I sometimes wondered if my father had suffered as much as I had with being an introvert.

My father died when he was 28, from injuries sustained in an automobile accident. I was still an unknown face in my mother's womb when he passed, but Mom named me after him to honor his memory.

Mom didn't talk about my father much, but certainly not because he was a terrible husband, who did awful things to her. It was quite the opposite; my father was a good man, who she missed greatly. I would sometimes catch her sobbing late at night, as she looked through old photographs of their wedding day. It killed me to witness Mom during these private moments, and so I avoided them when I could.

Mom wasn't alone for long though, and she remarried a few years later, to a man named William Jacobs. I was around six years old and still naïve to the world when Mom brought William home to meet me. The idea of having a father figure in my life was something that I only dreamt of, and from that day forward, William became the only father I had ever known. Unfortunately, William was not the sort of dad I envisioned when I thought of role model fathers. I suppose my idea of an ideal father figure was distorted by my beliefs that every head of the household, was like your typical sitcom dad.

Unfortunately for me, the Steven Keaton's, and the Ward Cleaver's of the world were only mirages on a big dumb box. William was not the sort of stepfather that would take you fishing, or to watch a ballgame on a Sunday afternoon. That's because William, was a functioning alcoholic—devoted to working his job as a security officer for the *DMV*—and drinking just enough alcohol to get him through the day. He didn't start his real drinking until he arrived home, when he usually downed a twelve pack of Old Milwaukee, while taking shots of Jim Beam and cursing at the Pittsburg Pirates on the RCA.

During his spare time, he was usually emotionally and physically abusive to Mom and me. She finally had enough of William's alcoholic, aggressive behavior, and asked for a divorce. This made William livid, to the point where his only response was to deposit his fist through the drywall of my mother's bedroom. Despite a restraining order against him, and being served with divorce papers, he continued to call our house daily, with tear-filled promises of changed behavior. My mother was fearful, and wanted to protect me, and it was the only reason why we were moving away from Scranton.

I just don't understand why we have to move to Maine. It could have been anywhere else and I would have been happy, but no, Mom had her heart set on Maine. There was no plan in moving, we just packed up what we could fit in the car, and left. My mother had a small savings, which she had been hiding from William, and she was going to use it to get us as far away from him as possible (her exact words). I always pictured myself living somewhere a bit more exotic and interesting. New York City, or even California, but those were just fantasies I had while lying in my bed at night. To a 15-year-old boy, Maine seemed to be one of the least interesting places on earth; nevertheless, we were on our way there now, and there was no turning back. Mom had been mostly quiet since we left Scranton this morning, barely taking her eyes off the road to look at me—other than to ask me if I needed to use the restroom. The distance between us was unbearable at times, both of us not knowing exactly what to say to comfort the other. I imagine this decision to move must have been a struggle for her, but I know her love for me was the compass that pointed us in this direction. It was just her and I from now on, much like when my father passed away and we struggled to make a life for ourselves. This was the struggle all over again, except this time, we were not just sad, but fearful as well.

We knew William to be a violent drunk—but would he find the determination to look for us in our new town? I felt that him looking for us seemed like a long shot, given his lack of enthusiasm for anything other than alcohol. But, if he did try, in some last desperate attempt to find us, I believe the played-out scenario would be something that I refer to as the three D'S: Drink, Drive, Die.

This comes from knowing that his driving was a reckless endeavor, due to a constant state of intoxication.

I can honestly say, I have never seen William sober since he has been in our lives. Mom did much of the driving for William, and the task of taking him to work, and the liquor store became a daily routine. I was not afraid of him finding us, but Mom seemed to be worried about what he would do if he found us living happily somewhere without him. I tried explaining to her, that he could barely find the balance to aim straight into the toilet, and that he would most likely crash and die, long before he reached the state line out of Pennsylvania. This brought her some comfort, but Mom has always been a worrier, and there was nothing I could say, or do, to change that.

Mom was an attractive woman of forty-three, with golden hair, sun kissed skin, and a contagious laugh, that would cause her nose to snort like a pig when she really got going. An only child, her mother named her Bethany, after her great grandmother, but she preferred to be called Beth. Her parents both passed away a few years ago, so she was alone now—except for me, of course.

I never knew what Mom saw in William, a man with the personality of a dried prune, and a face to match. He was only two years older than my mother, but years of smoking and drinking made him look considerably older. To say that they were an odd couple would be an understatement. It has always been my belief, that when my father died, Mom gave up on finding love again, by settling for the vilest human being she could find. I felt that Mom being with William, was her way of punishing herself for not being in the car with my father on that fateful night.

It was the only reasoning that made sense to me, to explain why such a smart, beautiful woman would ever consider marrying a jerk like William. It sure wasn't his charming personality that reeled my mother in, but whatever it was, he managed to convince her into marrying him.

I always pictured Mom with someone handsome, such as a Pierce Brosnan, or a Harrison Ford type. I secretly hoped that she would find love again, and that maybe, our new town would introduce her to some new people.

I didn't know much about our new town, other than it being close to the fishing docks, and that they held a carnival every Fourth of July. Mother was there once as a child, stopping with her family on the way to Acadia National Park for their annual family vacation. Although her stay at Sherbrook was short, she never forgot the quiet beauty of the town. The peaceful sounds of the waves beating against the rocky shore, and the smell of the salty air surrounding the town; at least that's how she described it to me. I found quiet beauty to be quite boring, and as much as I was not a people person, I still longed for the loud noises that only a big city could bring. Quietness hurt my brain, with intrusive thoughts, and memories of yesterday's regrets. I know it sounds silly, but I needed chaos in my life, to forget about the chaos in my life.

We have just reached the state line into Maine, and I can feel the anxiety creeping over my body. It feels as though I have been sitting in this car forever, but the watch on my wrist reminds me that it is only noon. Goodbye, New Hampshire, I say to myself, as we leave the state behind. I didn't actually see much of New Hampshire—other than a dirty truck stop, and what I managed to see flying by my window at 55mph. This is becoming a reality now, and what was once just a blank canvas in my brain a few hours earlier is now painting its landscapes into my mind.

The rain has stopped, and for the first time since we left Scranton, the sun appears to be breaking through the clouds. It was a promising sign, and Mom looked over at me and smiled, while turning the radio dial to some New Wave channel. "Are you getting hungry?" she asked. "There is a diner at the next exit and we can grab a bite to eat, if you'd like?"

It was the first time Mom had spoken to me in over an hour. She seemed calm and at ease, as the sun gleamed through the windows and onto her face, showing her age. Moving to Maine is not something I wanted, but I did enjoy seeing her happy.

"Yeah, I can eat," I said, "besides, I need new batteries for my Walkman."

"Ok, maybe we can look for a RadioShack or something."

My Walkman was my escape from reality. It helped to block out William, on nights, when all I could hear was him shouting at my mother in a drunken stupor, speaking in meaningless rambles, on anything from politics, to the black neighbors who lived across the street. The man had no filter when it came to unleashing his propaganda on the unwilling, but luckily for me, I had my Walkman to block out his dimwitted rhetoric.

Mom pulled off the exit and into the town of *Tall Oaks,* where we stopped at *Luke's Diner.*

The place looked as though it had been erected sometime during the First World War, and probably hadn't changed much since. The structure was a bizarre shaped atrocity, that appeared to be made from aluminum and tin, with a rusty old sign hanging on top, that read: *Luke's Diner.* I felt as though a tetanus shot was needed before entering, but what the hell—I was hungry. It was a quarter after twelve now, and despite the outside of the diner looking dilapidated, I was hoping the food would make up for the lack of curb appeal.

"Are we really that hungry to eat here?" Mom said, with a wary look on her face, as we stepped through the front door. She seemed to be half joking, but I couldn't be sure.

There was a musty odor to the place. An odor that comes from the smell of water that lay stagnant for an undetermined amount of time. It was evident to my nostrils, that the ventilation in this place was little to nonexistent. Two elderly gentlemen sat at the counter, smoking their Lucky Strikes, and observing us with glassy eyes. The place was humid, with no working air conditioner, and only a small ceiling fan that continued to blow dust and smoke amongst the small confines of the establishment.

A middle-aged woman came out from around the counter and greeted us with a smile, introducing us to her yellow, decaying teeth. "Sit anywhere you'd like, and I'll be with you shortly," she said, with a cigarette hanging from her lip. We moved to the back of the diner and found a booth by the window, hoping, that we could somehow avoid the lingering smoke that was circulating throughout.

I raised my eyebrows to my mother, as if to question our decision for stopping at such a place. After about two minutes, the waitress walked over to our table and handed us two menus.

"Welcome to Luke's Diner," she said, with an overly enthusiastic tone. "My name is Bridget, and I will be your server this afternoon. Can I start you off with something to drink? Perhaps a soda pop, or a freckled milkshake?"

I'd never heard of a freckled milkshake, and quite frankly, I was in no hurry to find out. My mother looked up from her menu and ordered a coffee, black, and a glass of water with no lemon.

"I'll have a can of Cola please," I said to the waitress as she took the orders, and retreated to the kitchen.

I usually ordered my soda in a glass, but I could see no reason to play daredevil in a diner that looked as though it was a former fallout shelter during the war.

"What are you hungry for?" Mom inquired.

"I don't know, everything looks so appetizing," I said with a hint of sarcasm. "I suppose anything that won't make me violently ill."

Mom smiled, and reminded me of Grandma Millie's house—where it always stunk of cooked cabbage and cigarettes—but whose delicious meatloaf dinners could turn any hardcore vegetarian into a raging carnivore. God, how I missed her meatloaf, I thought.

"How bout we just give the place a chance; who knows, perhaps this place is a diamond in the rough," Mom said with a smile.

The waitress returned with our beverages, and asked if we were ready to order. Mom ordered a turkey club with a side of French-fries. I played it safe, and ordered a grilled cheese with tomato soup. It seemed like a dish that even a disastrous cook such as myself would have difficulty in screwing up. The waitress scribbled something down in her notepad, thanked us, and walked away.

The whole diner seemed like something out of the Twilight Zone. A few local oddballs, sitting at a mysterious diner, in the middle of God knows where, seemed like the beginning of a mystery to me. It was a mystery I did not care to solve, and I most definitely did not want to be a part of it.

The men seated at the counter made me feel uneasy with their occasional stares, as they sipped their coffees and made incoherent chatter.

The whole thing was downright unnerving. Mom seemed more focused on her coffee cup, and whether the proportioning of her creamer was off balance with the consistency she was seeking. It seemed to me, that she had a lot more than coffee on her mind, as she stared blankly at her cup.

"Where are we going to stay when we get to Sherbrook?" I said, to break up the silence for a moment.

"I suppose we can stay at a motel for the night, and then look over the classifieds in the morning for a place to rent. I also need to look for a job," she said with a sigh.

Mom had always been a stay at home Mom, and never had a regular nine to five job—so, I could understand her frustration. She had always depended on my father, or William, to bring home the paycheck, while she worked around the house, cooking and cleaning—not to mention, trying to keep me out of trouble.

"I guess I can try to get a job as a waitress or a housekeeper," she said, trying to be optimistic. "Besides, those are the only things I have ever been good at."

"Things will work out," I said, "the main thing is we have each other."

She smiled, and put her hand over mine. I smiled back and embraced the moment.

The moment was quickly interrupted by the waitress approaching the table with our lunch.

"One grilled cheese on white with tomato soup for the boy, and a turkey club with fries for the lady," she said, as she set our meals down on the table. "Can I get you anything else, a refill perhaps?"

"No thanks," Mom said, without asking if I needed anything. "Well, I have to admit, the food does look edible, and dare I say, delicious."

I hesitantly picked up the grilled cheese sandwich and inspected it. No moldy breed, and from what I could tell, no bugs in my soup. That was good enough for me. I immediately dipped the grilled cheese into the tomato soup. The bread soaked up the tomato like a sponge, and melted the cheese into a creamy sauce. I took a bite, much too large for my mouth, as cheese dripped from the sandwich and onto my plate.

Mom took a bite of her turkey club, and we looked at each other, nodding in approval. The food turned out to be better than expected, but the people were another story. To say that they were creepy and weird, would be an understatement. I wondered if all the locals in Maine were this suspicious of outsiders.

We finished our lunch, and Mom excused herself to use the restroom. I noticed the men eyeballing her and whispering, as she walked by them.

I couldn't tell if they were checking her out because they thought she was attractive, or because they were simply suspicious of her character. I guess they would be right on both accounts, I thought, as I sipped the last of my soda. The last slurp of my straw echoed within the empty can, and was loud enough to draw their attention back to me, as I pretended not to notice. I sucked loudly on the straw a few more times, just to tick them off for being creepy old men, and smirked ever so slightly as I did. After a few minutes, Mom walked out of the restroom, and paid the bill. The old men sat there, silently watching like crows on a telephone line.

"Thank you, come again," the waitress said, as we walked away to leave.

When we arrived outside, Mom looked at me and said, "Was it just me, or were those old men being terribly rude by staring at us?"

I chuckled, unaware that Mom was more observant than I gave her credit for. "I didn't want to alarm you by saying anything in there, but yeah, they were staring," I said.

"I'm just glad to be out of there!" she exclaimed, as she rolled her eyes.

"Me too," I said, as I opened the passenger side door. The sweltering heat that had been trapped inside the car escaped across my body, and I took a step back. I was not prepared for this unique sort of heat that was more suitable for the Caribbean.

"I thought Maine was supposed to be cooler than this?" I said, as I wiped the beads of sweat from my forehead.

"Yeah, it does seem unusually hot for Maine, now that I think about it. You might as well enjoy it while it lasts, because Maine is known for its bone-chilling winters."

I suddenly pictured myself on a Florida beach, soaking up the sun's rays. God, I'm dreading Winter in Maine.

"This is the last stop before we get to Sherbrook," Mom said, as she pulled the map out of the glove compartment and pointed to our current location. "It should only be about 35 more miles, and then we will be in our new city, and starting our new lives."

It was hard to imagine another city and state making its imprint on my heart the way Scranton had. Scranton was as dull as any other city, I suppose, but I felt a certain attachment to the place—after all, I did invest fifteen years of my life there.

I leaned back into my seat with my Walkman on, when I realized that Bowie was singing slower than usual. "Mom, we need to stop for batteries; my Walkman is almost dead."

"How come you didn't remind me when we left the diner?" she huffed.

"C'mon, Ma, Bowie sounds like he is singing in subliminal messages."

"We can stop when we get to Sherbrook, besides, we only have a few miles to go, so just listen to the radio." She turned the radio dial to one of her Top 40 stations that I despised so much. I sighed, knowing all too well that I had lost this battle with Mom. Once she made up her mind, there was no point in arguing further. Mom might have taken William's crap on a daily basis, but she sure as hell wasn't about to answer to her 15-year-old son. I had learned over time, that it was never a good idea to argue with her, because I always lost—no matter if I believed I was right, or not.

The songs flickered with static and broken verses, as I took in the views from my window. The cars flew by us, as Mom complained about everyone else's driving. She had this habit of driving slower than the listed speed limit, and it drove me—along with everyone she shared the road with—crazy. Just once, I wanted to see her go over the speed limit.

I lounged back into my seat and closed my eyes, as I listened to the white noise of the radio, quietly whispering in my ears, as I drifted off to sleep.

Mom tapped me on the shoulder, as I wiped the drool from the side of my lip. "What time is it?" I said, as I blinked continuously, trying to adjust my eyes to the sun.

"It's time to get up," she said, as she handed me her sunglasses.

I took the sunglasses, fully aware that they were women's, and put them over my sleepy eyes. "I'm so tired," I said, with a yawn. I looked up and saw that we had stopped at a motel called the *Leisure Inn*.

"Wait here, I'm going to book us a room for the night," Mom said, as she stepped out of the car.

The once white paint on the walls of the motel had succumbed to the elements, and were in desperate need of a fresh coat. The place needed a full renovation, or maybe just a bulldozer. Two cars were parked outside, most likely belonging to the staff. Who in their right mind would want to stay at a place like this? I wondered.

A few anguished faces peered from their windows, as if they were uncomfortable to see new guests arriving for something other than sex or drugs. I hated the thought of sleeping on a bed, where numerous acts of God-knows-what had occurred. I pictured a floor covered in used syringes, and empty condom wrappers, left from *Johns*, and women looking to make a quick dollar.

I knew money was tight, but couldn't Mom find anything better than this?

After a few minutes, Mom walked out of the motel office, smiling, and dangling the keys of our new room in her hand. I reluctantly walked to the back of the car and removed my two burgundy suitcases, as I followed behind her.

"Here it is," she said, as she pointed to the door.

I looked up at the door, while trying to adjust my eyes to the blinding sun, and noticed it was room thirteen.

Oh God, I thought. Thirteen has always been a bad omen for me. I was born into this world fatherless, on the thirteenth day of October.

Thirteen was the number of students in my Science class that I failed miserably. And on my 13th birthday, William came home drunk from the bar and decided I was old enough at thirteen to challenge him in a game of drunk boxing—except this was no game. It was a match that had left me with two black eyes, a busted lip, and my body looking like a *Smurf* for two weeks.

He insisted it was a rite of passage into adulthood, and believed it would make me stronger—it didn't. When he sobered up, and saw the results of his actions all over my beaten body, he laughed. He then threatened, that if I ever told Mom about what had occurred, that her bruises would make mine look like mosquito bites. When Mom awoke the next morning, and saw me struggling to walk, she was livid. I had to lie to her, and made up some elaborate story, about a gang of neighborhood kids who had jumped me for $2.50, and my brand-new pair of Adidas shoes that she had recently bought me for my birthday. God, I loved those shoes, and it killed me to toss them into the dumpster for my lie to seem believable.

To this day, I never told her the truth about the incident, and I am sure she would have picked another room if she knew about my poisoned relationship with the number thirteen.

Mom eased the key into the lock and turned the doorknob, as I closed my eyes, imagining this was some five-star hotel resort that catered to the rich and famous. I shook my head and followed behind her as we entered the unlit room.

"Open those curtains and let's get some sun in here," she said, as she tossed her suitcase on the bed.

I yanked the curtains open, as the sun projected a sea of dust particles that seemed to dance throughout the room like little fairies making their escape from Neverland.

"So much for leaving a tip for the housekeeper," Mom said, trying to make light of the situation. I collapsed onto my bed and suddenly jumped back up, realizing that I hadn't checked for bed bugs. I recalled the story of young Jonathan Baily: a boy in my English class, who spent his Christmas vacation at *Lake George, New York*, and came home with a suitcase full of bed bugs. A notice was given to the students and faculty, after someone observed one of the insects around his book bag during lunch. Due to health hazards, he was banned from school until his parents hired an exterminator to get rid of them. When he finally returned to school after two weeks, his story had spread like wildfire throughout the halls of Scranton elementary. Once a semi-popular boy, who was starting to rise through the ranks of popularity—now he had become the target of constant ridicule and bullying. The bullying eventually had gotten so bad, in fact, that his parents had to send him to a private school out West, and I never heard of him, or his bed bugs ever again.

I have never been one to care about what others thought of me, but nevertheless, I did not want to start off my reputation in a new school with a label associated with bed bug infestation. I saw first-hand what that sort of thing could do to someone's school status, and I was not about to become a victim like the unfortunate Jonathan Baily. I have always managed to stay under the radar, and I preferred not to draw any unwanted attention from bullies just looking for an excuse to start trouble.

I carefully looked over the white sheets and blankets that appeared to have surrendered to the elements of the room's past tenants. Mom looked at me as if I had two heads, as I cautiously made my way around every inch of the mattress, while being ever so careful not to miss a spot. Dried drops of blood, cigarette burns, and what looked to be semen, or mucus, were scattered throughout the bed like a bullet-ridden blanket of human waste.

"I cannot sleep here. I have no idea what's on this bed, but I am not sleeping in it," I said, as I flung the sheets on the floor. I pointed to some dried-up spots of God only knows what. "This here is a breeding ground for parasites just looking for a host to attach itself to." Having literally read hundreds of comics about insects and parasites that had taken over entire cities, I believe I had enough knowledge to know, that it never ends well for the humans who have the unfortunate luck of running into them.

"C'mon Justin, work with me here. It's one night and that's it. I promise, no dirty motels after tonight," she said to me, as she gave me those damn puppy dog eyes.

Damnit, I hated when she gave me that look. She did that to me, knowing damn well that it gets me every time. "Fine," I said hesitantly, "but It doesn't mean I'm going to like it."

"I don't expect you to like it. I certainly don't, but we both have to start making sacrifices until we can get on our feet." Mom, grabbed a metal ice bucket lying on the floor, and handed it to me.

"What do you want me to do with this?"

"Go outside and see if you can find us some ice, and if you can't, then go to the office and ask the manager."

"Come on, Mom, can't it wait until later?"

She gave me this stern look and started to open her mouth to speak, but before she could say another word, I just said, "fine," and walked out.

I looked to my left and then to my right, to make sure that the path was cleared of junkies and weirdos. I heard some muffled bickering between two people, as I made my way slowly past the rooms of the motel. I noticed that each door was painted a different color, and that some of the rooms were missing the numbers on the front. "What a dump," I grumbled under my breath, as I made my way around the building.

The sun was especially unkind on the other side of the motel, where there seemed to be less shade, and less paint on the walls. It was a simmering heat, that caused me to sweat profusely from my forehead, and drip into my eyes. Hot enough to make my shirt stick to me like scotch tape. *I don't know why I expected Maine to be cooler, maybe it was something I read in a Steven King novel,* I thought.

"You lost, boy?" a raspy woman's voice called out to me, as I walked aimlessly in search of ice.

"Excuse me," I said, as my eyes searched for the source of the voice.

"In here, boy, room 21," the woman's voice called out once more.

I approached the room slowly, where I noticed the door slightly ajar, and a woman's eye gazing at me from within. "Don't be afraid—I don't bite," she said. Her iris, a cloudy grey, surrounded by puffy dark circles, and crow's feet radiated from the outer corner of her eye. "What's your name, son?" she said, as she opened the door slightly more.

"Justin," I said as I stumbled backwards a bit. "My mother and I, are staying on the other side of the building in room thirteen. You wouldn't happen to know where I could find an ice machine around here, would you?" I held up the empty bucket and the woman gazed at it for a moment before opening the door. The smell of burning incense lingered through the breeze, and rushed up through my nostrils, causing me to bellow out a hefty sneeze. "Aww Choo."

I looked up to see a mahogany skinned woman standing before me, her best days far behind her, with a black eraser size mole on her left cheek— that I couldn't seem to take my eyes off. She clutched her ebony cane with her weathered hands, that appeared to have seen their fair share of hard labor throughout the years. A faded tropical Mumu, embraced her disproportioned body, as she leaned in like a hunchback to greet me.

"My name is Amelia," she said. "Now what can I do for you?"

"Huh… but you called out to me," I said, slightly confused.

"Yes, but you're lost. I can tell when someone is lost. It's the kind of thing that sort of becomes second nature when you been around as long as I have. Why don't you come in for a moment, and we will discuss your problem. I might have the answers that you seek." And with that, she turned around, and headed back into her room without saying another word.

"I really can't stay," I said. "If you could just point me in the direction of the nearest ice machine, I sure would appreciate it. My mother is expecting me any minute now with some ice, and if I'm not back soon, she's going to give me hell."

"She can wait, Justin. What I have to tell you is far more important than a bucket of ice." She motioned for me to come inside, almost hypnotically.

I gradually walked in, with my curiosity leading the way. I was intrigued enough by what she wanted to tell me, and curious, about the candles and tarot cards placed on her table, that I managed to get a glimpse of while rubbernecking over her shoulders.

"Close the door, and let us have some tea," she said, as she looked back and smiled.

I closed the door. "I'm not much of a tea drinker; do you have anything cold?"

"Nonsense," she said, "everyone loves tea. Now sit down anywhere you'd like—except here." She pointed to a worn-out recliner. "My body is not what it used to be. It's the only chair that makes sitting somewhat comfortable for my old bones."

I walked past the recliner and over to the couch where I sat down. "Wow, this is some interesting stuff you have here. I have never seen so many mystical objects outside of a museum."

"Oh, I doubt you'd find any of these things inside a museum, Justin. Would you like milk or sugar in your tea," she said, as she glanced over her shoulder.

"Sugar, please."

"Will two teaspoons suffice?"

"Yeah, whatever," I said, as I picked up one of the tarot cards that had the words *The Fool* written on it. Books on candle rituals and spells were scattered throughout the shelves of the small room. Three large dreamcatchers hung from the ceiling, and crystals and amulets were placed meticulously around what appeared to be animal bones.

"Hey, don't touch that. Those are not toys," she scolded.

"Sorry, but what is all this stuff?"

12

"Enchanted objects and spells mostly," she said as she handed me my tea. "Most of what you see here is what I use to ward off evil spirits."

"Negative energy, from this world, and one which never existed."

"Negative energy?" I said as I took a sip of my tea.

"Evil is all around us, Justin. Some evil we can see for ourselves on the nightly news, and some evil." She paused for a moment to take a sip of her tea before continuing. "Well… some evil hides in the darkest corners of the earth, just waiting for someone to release it. You on the other hand—you have known evil in the flesh."

"What are you talking about?"

"You have a gift—one that comes not of this world, but a world that is incomprehensible to those with closed minds."

"I'm afraid you're mistaken; I don't possess any gifts." I placed my teacup on the table and got up to leave.

"Oh, but you do, dear. I saw your aura as you walked by my door."

"My what?" I asked, as I attempted to leave.

"Your aura. A light that surrounds you—a third eye if you will."

"Thanks for the tea, but all I really need is some ice."

"Just listen to what I have to say-"

"No offense, but I don't want anything to do with your spells or witchcraft."

"Is that what you think this is? Witchcraft? I am no witch, I am many things, but a witch is not one of them."

"I appreciate your concern, I really do, but I must be going." I held up the ice bucket and proceeded to walk out the front door.

"I will be here when you are ready," she said, as I made my way towards my room.

I arrived at my room, slightly out of breath, and shaken a bit by the odd circumstances that had unfolded in room 21. What gift could I possible have? I thought. The old woman was obviously not in touch with reality to think that I possessed any sort of gift. I stared at the faded number *13* on the door, which seemed to have already planted its malicious seed into my life.

"Oh crap," I said, as I looked down at the empty ice bucket.

Mom was going to kill me, but I was not about to explore this cesspool any further tonight. I slowly turned the doorknob and entered.

.

2. GIFT OR CURSE?

Mom was asleep in her bed when I entered the room, and didn't seem to notice, as I stumbled over her shoes. I extend my arms, trying to grab the bed for support, but quickly lost my balance and fell face first onto the burnt orange carpet. The loud thud of the impact must have surely woken her up, I thought—but it didn't. The scent of the carpet was a nauseating odor that Merriam-Webster would have found difficulty in defining. The rug was horribly tainted, and I was almost certain it had probably outlived its manufacturers and installers.

I picked myself up off the floor, and quietly laid down on my bed. I wasn't sure what the old woman in room 21 wanted to talk to me about, or what her story was, but I wanted no part of it either way. Who in their right mind keeps animal bones and spell books in their house anyway? Besides, if she really could tell the future and see things, then why is she staying at some half a star motel in the middle of Maine?

Don't get me wrong, I love reading about the unknown and things that go bump in the night, but it's still just fantasy to me. An escape from reality, when each passing day becomes more mind-numbing than the last. There is no truth to the stories that I read. I don't believe in monsters living in lagoons, or vampires living in castles halfway across the world, feeding off human blood from silver goblets. As clever as those stories are, they are still just that: stories to entertain the mind.

I moved my pillow a bit to get comfortable as the rickety bed squeaked below me.

"Oh, you're back," Mom said. "Did you get the ice?"

"I couldn't find the ice machine; I don't even think they have one."

"You don't think, or you didn't ask?"

I stood there silent while I bit my lip nervously. Mom glowered at me suspiciously.

"Did you talk to the office manager like I asked you to, or not?"

"No, but I did bump into this weird old lady that kind of freaked me out. So… I guess I sort of forgot about the ice and just ran back here instead."

Mom shot me a look of disbelief. "My God, Justin. I ask you to do me one little favor and you can't even do that for me." She reached for her Reeboks lying on the floor and pushed her feet in them without untying the laces.

"Why do we need ice anyway?" I said. "It's not like we have food to keep cold."

"Well, in case you haven't noticed, the air conditioner is broken and it's like 100 degrees in here," she said. "I thought it would be nice to fill up the tub with ice water, and take a bath."

"Maybe if you spent a little more money on a better motel, then we wouldn't have to take baths in buckets of ice. This whole half-assed decision to move to Maine, was your idea to begin with. News flash, Mom—I was perfectly happy with my life in Scranton—so why don't you get your own damn ice." I regretted the words as quickly as they came out of my careless mouth. Mom stood there with this staggered look on her face for a moment, before grabbing the ice bucket, and storming out the door. "Ugh, I hate this place!" I screamed.

I laid in bed for what seemed to be an eternity, replaying the day over and over in my head until I fell asleep.

I awoke to a bag of McDonalds being thrown onto my lap, and my mother's voice saying, "Wake up, you need to eat."

"What is it?" I asked, as I tried to get my thoughts together.

"Two cheeseburgers, no pickle, fries, and a Cola with light ice."

"Thanks, I'm starving," I said, as I discarded the wrapper around my cheeseburger and took a bite.

We both ate in an awkward silence for a few minutes, as I tried to figure out the best way to apologize for my selfish behavior earlier. I guess I better just say something, I thought.

"I'm sorry about what I said before, I didn't mean it. It's just that, well… I'm an idiot."

"You're not an idiot-insensitive maybe-but definitely not an idiot," she said with a slight smile.

"Besides, it all worked out for the best."

"What do you mean?" I asked.

"Well, while you were here snoozing, I made a few phone calls, and It looks as though I might have found us a place to live."

"Get out. Are you serious?" I said, standing up from my bed.

"While you were sleeping, I was down the street at a place called, *Carney's Doughnuts*—who happens to sell the worst coffee that I ever tasted. So, I'm drinking my lousy coffee, and I notice they had the local paper lying on the table. So, I started looking over the classifieds section for a place to rent. I called this place about a mile away from here, and talked to the nice old man who is renting it, and to make a long story short—we move in tomorrow."

"Awesome," I said, with my mouth filled with fries. My mind was in overdrive, as the questions came out faster than Mom could answer. "Where is it? What does it look like? Is my bedroom big? Is there a big yard?"

Mom shook her head and said, "You're giving me a headache. You can see for yourself tomorrow morning when we check out of this dump."

I grinned. "Oh, so you finally agree with me that this place is a dump?"

"Yeah, I do, but I had to budget ourselves so we could afford a real home of our own, and did I mention, it's fully furnished."

"Are you serious?" I said, a fry hanging from my lip like a cigar.

"Sometimes we need to make sacrifices, Justin. It's the only way people like us will ever get ahead."

"I know," I said, still feeling somewhat ashamed for questioning my mother's decision earlier. I knew she was doing her best under the circumstances. It's not like we came from a wealthy family where we had unlimited funds. I should be more reasonable, and realize, that everything she has been doing up to this point, was out of love for me.

"I won't ever question your decisions again," I said, as I walked over and gave her a hug. "Unless you decide to go back with William, then I might have to question your sanity."

"Oh, that's funny," she said with a "hardy har--har," and then looked at me serious and said, "I love you."

"I love you too, Mom," I said, as I hugged her once more, only tighter.

"Ok, you're killing me," she said, as she gasped for air. "Now let's get some sleep. Tomorrow is going to be a busy day."

I awoke from a nightmare that I could not recall, my body soaked in sweat, still trembling with fear. I looked over at the small clock on the nightstand that illuminated 5:05 a.m. The curtain allowed the faintest speck of light from the street lamp to shine through. It was just enough light to make out the silhouette of my mother, who was still fast asleep in her bed. I gathered my thoughts and tried to remember the details of my nightmare. Dammit, I know it was awful, but why can't I remember anything? I rarely dream, and I never have nightmares—at least not since I was around six years old, and still believed that the boogie man lived in my closet. I don't usually eat fast food before bed—could it have been that? Perhaps it had something to do with that psychic woman and her room full of oddities? She could have poisoned my tea—it did taste sort of strange. Maybe I was just being paranoid about the whole thing.

I made my way out of bed, and pushed the curtain aside to reveal some light making its way through the twilight sky. I remember reading an article about Maine in *National Geographic* when I was about ten, and how it was the first state to see the sunrise, and thinking how cool that was.

"What are you doing up?" Mom said, still half-asleep. "Are you that excited about the move today?"

"Yeah, but that's not the reason. I just had a bad dream and couldn't fall back to sleep."

"What was the dream about?"

"I don't remember."

"It probably has something to do with sleeping in a strange place," Mom said. "Your father was the same way— he could never get comfortable sleeping anywhere but his own bed."

"Yeah, you're probably right."

"Well, I guess I better get up," Mom said, stretching her arms out over her head, "I'm not going to be able to fall back asleep now. I'm going to take a shower, and then maybe we can check out of here and grab some breakfast. How does that sound?"

"Sounds like a plan," I said, still preoccupied with remembering the nightmare, and staring vacantly at the ceiling.

Mom grabbed a few things from her suitcase, before heading into the bathroom. "Do you have to use the toilet before I get undressed?" she said, from the other side of the door.

"No, but I think I am going to take a walk around the building to get some fresh air. I'll be back in five minutes."

"Okay, just don't be gone too long."

I slipped my black high tops over my feet and open the door as the morning air instantly surrounds my body, and waked my senses. The crisp breeze felt fresh and invigorating after spending the night in a room that felt like a sauna. I walked past the mostly quiet rooms of the motel until I reached room 21. I felt an urge to knock on the door and confront the old woman, but what would I say? I can't go accusing her of putting spells on me, besides, I don't even believe in that nonsense, or at least that's what I told myself. I bet it's all those horror comics and movies that have etched themselves into my memory that are causing me to have these delusional thoughts. I paced back and forth outside room 21, debating about whether to knock on the door, when suddenly, it opened. Amelia stood there, still wearing the same clothes as when I first met her, and smoking a clove cigarette which emitted an odor reminiscent of Mom's baked Christmas ham.

"Good morning, Justin," she said, as the ashes from her cigarette fell to the concrete.

I stood there mute, my eyes fixated on the mole on her left cheek, and trying desperately to comprehend what she was saying.

"Dear, you are being incredibly rude. The polite thing to say to someone who has just spoken good morning to you, would be good morning back."

"Now, let try this again. Good morning, Justin."

"Good morning," I said as I slowly started to get my thoughts together.

"See, that wasn't so hard now, was it?"

"I'm sorry, it's been a long night. I… um… just wanted to say goodbye."

No, that's not what I wanted to say at all. I wanted to tell her about the nightmare, and how I believe she drugged my tea with one of her potions, and how the mole on her left cheek made me anxious—but I didn't.

Her smile turned to disappointment. "Oh, you are leaving us, dear, I'm sad to see you go."

"It's not often we get visitors from out of town here at the inn, and we certainly don't get any with the gifts that you possess."

Oh great, I thought, *again with the gifts*.

"I have been living at this motel for, oh… let's see… I say, thirteen years now."

There it is again, I thought. Unlucky number thirteen, and now it made sense, as to why I got a funny vibe around her. The number seemed to make its way into my life in more times than I can remember.

"Most people come and go, but I'm too old to start over again. I imagine I'll die in this room, but that's hopefully not for another twenty years. Anyway, I won't hold you up, but if you ever want to stop by and visit an old woman, then don't hesitate to do so. My door is always open."

"Thanks, but I really must be going. It's a busy day for us," I said, as I turned to walk away, without looking back.

I arrived at my room, and from the outside, I can slightly hear Mom singing, Joan Jett, horribly out of tune. I walked in to find her with towels wrapped around her body and hair, and singing, or should I say— attempting to sing into her curling iron.

"What are you doing? I could hear you from outside," I said, trying hard not to laugh.

"Just having a little fun. Why? what's wrong with that?"

"Nothing. I just haven't seen this side of you in a long time."

It was nice to see my mother coming out of her shell once again.

I missed this woman—this was the mother I knew. The woman that was with William was a shadow of her former self. William broke my mother down by taking her personality and voice, and attempting to make it his own. She was not allowed to like or dislike something on her own free will. William made all the decisions for her. Breakfast at eight, lunch at twelve, dinner at five, and bedtime, no later than ten thirty on weekdays, and eleven on weekends. We both lived under William's rules and curfews for years, and now, here we were, in another state, just making the rules up as we go.

"C'mon and pack, I want to be out of here within twenty minutes, so jump to it," she said.

"Believe me, I don't want to stay here any longer than I have to."
I grabbed my clothes tossed about on the floor, and shoved them into my suitcase. "I'm going to brush my teeth and then we can go," I said.
"Aren't you going to take a shower before we leave?" Mom said.
"No, I will take one when we get to the new place. I don't
want to spend another second in this motel with its strange cast of characters."
I grabbed my toothbrush from my travel bag and put it in my mouth as I walked to the bathroom, which was big enough for only one person, covered in mildew and stinking of stale air. The mirror was covered with years of grime, and allowed about fifty percent visibility, as I stared at my blurred reflection. I opened the small, complimentary, mint fresh toothpaste that the motel provided. It looked to be well past its expiration date judging by the texture of it, but with a little squeeze, it landed like cement onto my brush.
"Oh, disgusting."
The fresh mint taste that once occupied the tube was long gone, and I was left with an awful taste of cheap medicine. I gargled and spit, and repeat, and it seemed to somewhat dissipate the lingering taste in my mouth. I looked at myself closely in the mirror and noticed a small red zit forming on my chin. "Oh, that's just great," I said as I squeezed it and splashed my face with cold water. "Ok, let's get out of here," I said, still drying my face with the bathroom towel.
"I put the bags in the car while you were brushing your teeth, so I will just hand in the keys, and then we can get out of here," Mom said.
"Thank God, I will wait for you in the car."
I walked to the car and pulled the handle to open the door and the heat surrounded me like a brick oven. Damn, maybe once Mom gets on her feet, we can afford a car with a working air conditioner. I slowly rolled down all the windows in the car, as the handles squeaked noisily away. Relief, not much, but it was still better than nothing. I leaned back into the seat and looked over my shoulder to catch a glimpse of Amelia, struggling with a bag, as she made her way to the dumpster. I wondered what hid behind the darkness of those bags: dead animals, human skulls, evidence of crimes committed with black magic? On second thought—I don't want to know. If this were 1692, the old woman would have been burned alive at the stake for what she was doing in that room. I was just relieved that I wouldn't have to spend another night in this dump with the freak show that was happening in room *21*. Mom startled me as she opened the car door and told me to buckle up—and with that—we were on our way to our new house.

"So, what do you want for breakfast," Mom asked.

"Can we please skip any diners today? No offense, but after that last diner experience, I think fast food would be our best option."

Mom smirked. "But I thought you enjoyed the food at the diner?"

"I didn't like it enough to go back there—now can we please just eat at McDonalds today?"

"You and your fast food. You know that stuff is going to kill you if you keep eating it."

"Well, at least I will die happy."

Mom pulled the car into the McDonalds parking lot, and headed for the drive thru window, where she ordered two egg McMuffins, and two large orange drinks. Mom didn't need to ask anymore what I wanted when it came to McDonalds breakfast. After ordering the same thing, time after time—it just became obvious. Mom pulled some money from her purse and paid the cashier, and after about two minutes, she handed us our food and drinks, and we drove away.

I was feeling dehydrated, and decided to drink my juice first. My mom fumbled with the wrapper of her sandwich, while trying to drive and eat at the same time.

"Be careful, I'd like to see my sixteenth birthday."

"I can eat and drive at the same time. I've been doing this for years."

"Yeah, but not well."

"Ha, very funny. Wait until you get your license and have kids. You remember my words—there will come a time when you will be juggling many task, and you're going to find yourself multitasking, all because there are not enough hours in a day."

"Fine, I believe you—now just keep your eyes on the road."

"Just eat your breakfast," she said as she laid her sandwich down on the dash to turn on the radio.

The *Boomtown Rats* were playing on the station, and I smiled, because it's one of those bands that had one hit years ago, then you kind of forget about them, until one day, you hear the song and you're like—yes—this song rocks.

She went to switch the station to another and I grabbed her hand to stop her. "Please, Mom, I like this song."

"Okay--Okay, you can listen to it, as long as you don't lecture me on my driving anymore."

"Deal," I said, knowing full well that I would criticize again tomorrow.

3. WELCOME TO THE NEIGHBORHOOD

"So, are you excited?" Mom asked.

"Are you kidding me? I can't wait. I just hope we don't get stuck with uptight neighbors."

"From what the landlord described to me on the phone, the houses are not close to one another. If anything, you might have to walk around to find someone to play with."

"I don't play anymore, Mom—I'm fifteen—I hang out. Playing is what toddlers do."

"Oh, I'm sorry. I forgot that you are a man now," she said, as she patted my head.

"I said I'm a man, not a dog." We both smiled and laughed. I love my mother this way; uncontrolled with no filter, and doing her own thing.

My mother had been trapped under William's spell for so long, that I almost forgot who my real mother was. This is her, this is the woman my father fell in love with before everything fell apart.

"Your father would have been proud of you," she said, while briefly taking her eyes off the road.

"Oh yeah. Why's that?"

"Because you're a good kid, and you never really give me a hard time about most things."

"Thanks," I said, feeling somewhat embarrassed.

"You know… even when William was being a jerk; you never gave him any lip, because you didn't want to enrage him. You're smart like that. You know people, and you know when to keep your mouth shut."

"Believe me, I wanted to tell him off, but I was scared. I wasn't brave, Mom, I was a coward."

"Well, I beg to differ," she said. "Sometimes the bravest thing a person can do is keep their mouth shut. Remember: any fool can argue about anything, but it takes someone strong to hold their tongue to a fool."

"Where did you hear that from?"

"Your grandmother. She was a wise woman your nana."

"Yeah, so I heard."

Mom pulled the directions the landlord gave her out of the glove compartment, while steering the car with one hand. "Now, if my calculations are correct, then we should be making a left onto Ember Drive, and then the house should be on our right."

The neighborhood was more country than I had imagined, with tall trees, and open fields that separated the homes with large gaps.

"Its 348 Willow Drive—keep an eye out for a white house with brown shutters," Mom said.

"There it is," I said, as I tugged on her shirt and pointed repeatedly out the window. My excitement could hardly be contained. The house was an old Victorian, in desperate need of a landscaper. The grass was overgrown, and brown bushes were lined up in front of the house like dead soldiers. The driveway was made of cracked cobblestone, with weeds growing out of every crevice. Despite the rundown appearance, the house had a certain charm about it. It's as if the house was calling out to me, and I could hear its welcoming whispers in my ear. The house was broken, but then again, so were we. One could say it needed us, just as much as we needed it. We pulled to the end of the driveway, and my mother put the car in park.

There was an old man and woman sitting on a pair of rocking chairs on the front porch. They looked to be around eighty years old, but probably no older than seventy-five.

"How do you do?" the old man asked, while rocking back and forth and puffing on a wood-cherry, calabash pipe.

"We are fine," my mother said, as she approached the couple with her hand extended. The old man shook her hand, as the old woman continued rocking as if we weren't there.

"You the woman I talked to on the phone about renting the house?" the old man said.

"Yes, that would be me. I'm Beth, and this is my son Justin."

"Nice to meet you both—I'm Henry, and this is my wife, Mary."

"Just let me grab my walking stick and I will show you two around."

The old woman rocked silently in her chair, staring off into the distance, as if seeing something only she could see.

"Don't mind Mary," Henry said, "she is partially deaf, and got a bit of dementia. She has her good days and her bad days. Today... not so good."

"So, do you two live on the property?" Mom asked.

"Nah, we live up the roads a bit. Three miles north of here to be exact. This house has been in our family for generations. The old tenants moved out about six years ago, and it's gotten to be too much work for Mary, and I. The place needs a few things, but it's a solid home. The foundation is strong and will probably be standing a lot longer than I will."

The old man reached for an ebony cane perched against the wall, and wobbled a bit before catching his balance.

"You don't see architecture like this anymore," Mom said.

"Nope, you most certainly don't," Henry said, "and you won't find another around here with as much charm as this old house."

"Yeah, so why is the rent so cheap?" Mom inquired.

"The reason why it's so cheap is because it needs a lot maintenance," the old man said. "I assume you and your son will tend to its needs?"

"Of course," Mom said, while looking back at me.

"Grass will need to be cut, maybe a coat of paint here and there, and you, and your son here, should have yourself a beautiful home. Now come follow me and I'll show you around."

I walked behind the old man patiently, as I waited for him to slowly make his way into the house. I didn't need a tour of the home to decide if I wanted to live there.

I knew in my heart that this was the place where I wanted to wake up every morning. I walked into the living room, where the wooden floors made a harsh, high-pitched sound with each step.

I guess sneaking out in the middle of the night to explore the neighborhood was out of the question. The house had a distinctive odor, smelling dull and grassy, like an old library book. I knew the scent well, because it was the same smell that surrounded my Grandma Millie's home. I found the smell to be comforting, much like the pages of an old novel that survived decades of readers—the house had been lived in and survived.

The house was furnished, but with plastic covering most of the furniture, it made it nearly impossible to see what was underneath.

"Wow, would you look at that fireplace," Mom said, as she tapped me on the shoulder.

"Yes, the fireplace," the old man said, "I don't remember when it's been used last, but I wouldn't recommend using it until you can afford a chimney sweep."

"It's beautiful, and look at the detailed carvings in the wood mantle," Mom said.

"The house has three bedrooms, and two bathrooms, but I can't make it up those steps," the old man said, as he clutched his cane for support.

"Why don't you two look around without me, and then you can meet me on the front porch when you are done checking out the place."

"Okay, thank you," Mom said.

The old man struggled to find balance with his cane, as he moved unsteadily from side to side, until he reached the front porch.

"So, what do you think?" Mom asked, "should we go explore the rest of the house?"

"I love this house," I said, "I still can't believe we are going to be living here.

"Don't say you love it until we check out the rest of the place, but yeah, it's pretty cool. I'm going to check out the kitchen," she said, "so why don't you go upstairs and pick out a bedroom."

"Any bedroom I want? Even the biggest one?"

"Yes, just don't leave me sleeping in a closet."

I smiled and sprinted up the spiral, wooden staircase to find my new room. I could see an open door at the top of the steps, and I decided to make it my first stop. The room was small, perhaps it was used as a child's room. There wasn't much room for anything, but maybe a crib and a dresser. I already knew Mom was not going to want this room, and I certainly didn't want it, so I walked down the hall a bit to see room number two. This room was considerably larger, and fully furnished, with an antique, queen size bed, a dresser, and a small bathroom connected to it.

I wanted this room badly, but that was just me being selfish. Besides, I'm not a kid anymore, and it's time I started thinking about other peoples' needs. I walked out to check out room number three around the corner. The door was open and I poked my head in slowly, afraid to look and discover this room to be smaller than the first. The room was only slightly smaller than room number two, furnished with a twin-size bed, and an oak dresser. An antique mirror hung from the faded white walls, and the ceiling was high enough for me to jump and still not be able to reach the top.

This is more my style, I thought. Not big, but not small either. It had a cozy feel to it. I rested down on the bed, as it squeaked loudly beneath my body. The mattress was firm, and I pictured myself reading comics here under a dim light at night. I could hear footsteps approaching and quickly rose to my feet.

Mom peeked her head into the room, and smiled. "So, I see you found your new bedroom." I went to hug her, embracing her tightly around her waist. "What's that for?"

"I just wanted to say I love you. I know I don't say it much but… I really think you are pretty amazing."

My mother's eyes started to swell up as a few tears trickled down her cheeks. "You're making me cry," she said, as she held me tighter.

"I love you too, Justin, and no matter what happens—from this day forward—we are a team, and we will never let a man come between us ever again."

"Or a girl," I said.

"Or a girl," she said, still fighting back tears. Mom pulled the rent money out of her pocket and waved it in the air. "So, what do you think? Are we really doing this?"

"I think this might be the only thing I'm sure of," I said.

"So, it's a done deal. Let's go tell Henry that he just found himself some new tenants."

"You go ahead. I'll meet you downstairs in a bit; I want to check out the attic."

"Okay, just be careful up there."

The attic door was connected to the ceiling with a small shoestring attached to it. I grabbed the string and yanked down, as the ladder fell hard, nearly hitting my face. "Dammit!" I said, as I fell backwards, landing on my buttocks. My heart was beating so loud that I thought, at any second, it would burst out of my chest. I looked up, and saw nothing but darkness above me. I dusted myself off and looked around to make sure no one was witnessing this fiasco of chutes and ladders.

I cautiously reached for the ladder once again, as I carefully ascended the steps until my head was completely inside the attic. I felt around the darkness with my right hand, while using my left hand to steady myself on the ladder, until I felt a string between my fingers, and gave it a slight tug. The room lit up for a moment before flickering out to darkness. "Son of a bitch," I said.

"Hey, watch your mouth," Mom called.

"How long have you been standing there spying on me?" I said.

"Long enough to hear that foul mouth of yours. You know better than to use that language around me."

"But you weren't around," I said sarcastically, "you were downstairs, and I almost killed myself up here."

"Never mind, smartass, now get down here. You can explore the attic another time."

"I'm coming--I'm coming," I said, as I reluctantly stepped down the ladder. "So, what's for dinner?"

"If I hear you use that language again, it's going to be a bar a soap."

"I'm 15, and I hate to break it to you, but this is how 15-year old's talk."

"I don't care, you're smarter than that. You're not some street kid— you're a Spencer—and Spencer's choose their words carefully."

"Fine, what would you have me say when I get hurt? It's just an instinct Ma—when bad things happen—bad words are bound to follow."

"Just try and clean it up a bit next time."

"Fine, I will try to be more aware of my language."

If she only knew how often I cursed when she wasn't around, I'd probably be grounded until my eighteenth birthday.

William could say the F word a hundred plus times a day, and it wouldn't bother her, but if I said it—it was as if I broke every commandment in the book. When I was about ten years old, I stubbed my toe against the dining room table, and out came the Lord's name in vain. If you could have seen the look on my mother's face—it was if I put the nails into Jesus's cross myself.

After two months of being grounded, I learned my lesson well enough to keep the curses amongst friends only.

"Well, I'm still hungry, so if it's going to be soap for dinner, then you better get on with it."

"You must be feeling at home, because you're getting to be quite the jokester," she said, as we both walked downstairs.

"No, but seriously, I'm starving."

"Well, how does *KFC* sound?" she said. "I believe we passed one on our way here."

"Yeah, that sounds good, but do you mind picking it up? I have seen enough of the car for one day."

"Yeah, go ahead and relax," she said, as I tossed her the car keys.

"Thanks, Mom."

"Yeah, just try not to burn the house down while I'm gone—and stay out of the attic until I can get new lightbulb," she said, as she closed the door behind her. The noisy engine of her car started up, as I watched her drive away, and then: quiet.

I walked over to the television that was shielded in dust and turned the knob.

The old box flickered with static, as I contorted the antenna to various positions in hopes of getting some sort of signal. I shut it off after a few failed attempts and turned my attention to the kitchen window overlooking the backyard. The yard was a vast woodland of greens and browns, with mixes of weeds and bushes that seemed to lead into a never-ending forest of Pines. Wow, you won't find this in the city, I thought. It was quiet and secluded. A kind of place that was as picturesque as any painting that I had ever seen. No loud trains in the distance, no shouting or music to be heard; no noise pollution at all—other than the occasional insect or bird chirping slightly in the distance. This was a scene that my eyes and ears were not accustomed to—this was paradise.

The sky was turning grey outside, and I could hear the rumble of thunder in the distance. The wind picked up and rattled the windows as I stared hypnotically at the old weathervane spinning on top of the outdoor shed. I had an urge to go outside and wander the woods in the back of the house, but it was getting dark, and I was much too hungry to do proper exploration at the moment. I decided to wait until morning when I had a proper night's sleep—one that didn't include an automobile or a run-down motel.

Tonight, I was sleeping in my new room. Sure, it didn't have any of my little touches of comic books scattered about, and *Cure* posters on the wall—but all in good time.

After about thirty minutes of my stomach growling, I heard Mom's car pulling up into the driveway.

My mouth started to salivate, as I pictured the Colonel's crispy chicken on my plate. I ran to the door to let her in, but not out of being polite. No, this had more to do with my own selfish need for fried food and mashed potatoes.

"Looks like it's going to storm," Mom said, as she handed me a bag of chicken. "Why don't you set the table—there are paper plates and plastic utensils in the bag."

I set the table, we ate, chatted about our new place a bit, and decided to call it a night. "Don't worry about the mess," Mom said, "we can clean it up tomorrow."

"Don't worry, I'm not," I said with a chuckle. I walked lethargically up the steps to my bedroom, half exhausted from the day, and half weighed down with double portions of chicken and potatoes.

"Goodnight, and sleep well," Mom said.

"Yeah, goodnight," I said, as I turned the corner into my bedroom. A flash of lightning illuminated my entire room for no more than a brief second. My body, exhausted from the day, collapsed into the bed, as the rain started to pitter-patter against my window pane. Slow at first, and then heavy, as I closed my eyes, and fell asleep.

I awoke several hours later to a light thump on my window, and sat up in my bed, confused. The rain that had beat heavily upon the house earlier, was now just a slight drizzle. I looked around the room that was somewhat visible, thanks to the slight sliver of moonlight that managed to break away from the clouds. I reached for my swatch lying on my nightstand to check the time. The digital watch flashed 3:45 a.m, as I put it back down and rubbed my sleepy eyes.

The room grew quiet again, and I passed the whole thing off as nothing more than another odd dream. I lay back down and closed my eyes, but after a few silent minutes, I heard it again. "THUMP." Startled, I opened my eyes. It sounded like someone, or something was outside my window. I trembled with fear, and my breathing became heavier, as I clutched my blanket against my chest, as if it were some sort of shield. Was someone attempting to break into the house? The very house that has been abandoned fed the last six years, and assumed to still be empty. I reached for the small table lamp from the nightstand, in the hope of using it against whoever, or whatever was attempting to get into my room.

Step by step, I slowly inched my way towards the window, with the lamp in my right hand, slightly afraid to look and discover what was causing the noise. "THUMP".

I jumped back, as I saw what appeared to be a small pebble, ricocheting off my window. Ok, so now I know it's not an animal, because as far as I knew, animals did not throw stones. Unless Maine had some super species with extraordinary intelligence that I was unaware of—then this had to be a human. Now I was frightened, because I knew that whatever was outside my window, was an intelligent being, and not just some mindless animal looking for food. I gathered my courage, and with lamp still in hand, peeked out the window to the ground below.

At first, I didn't see anything, but as I looked more closely around the yard, I notice a beautiful girl lost within the tall grass. She looked to be around my age, with porcelain skin, enhanced by the shimmering moonlight.

Chestnut colored hair laid flat on her shoulders of her denim jacket. She smiled when she saw me, and waved at me to come down. *This is insane,* I thought. It must be a dream, or a bad joke. What could she possibly want with me at this hour? For a moment, I thought that maybe this was some sort of a ploy to get me outside, and as soon as I did, I would be pummeled by a gang of thieves. But there was something about her face that made her seem innocent—like she never did anything bad in her life. I waved at her, and showed her one of my fingers, in a gesture that meant one minute. I knew she couldn't hear me, but I had hoped she would get the gist of what I was trying to say. As I put the lamp back on the table, and attempted to go downstairs, I suddenly remembered the creaky wood steps.

Oh God, how am I going to get down the stairs without Mom waking up? Maybe I should try climbing out the window, although, I've never been much of a climber. I remember this one time during gym class my freshman year, how our instructor wanted the class to climb these thick ropes to the top in under a minute. I was just about to reach my goal, when I felt my gym shorts slipping down past my buttocks. In a panic, I attempted to pull them up, with one hand reaching for my shorts, and the other holding on to the rope. My grip became weak, and I fell onto the mat. The whole gymnasium erupted in a roar of laughter. I looked to the left of me and saw my gym shorts lying on the ground. It suddenly became obvious why everyone was laughing. All my underwear was dirty in the hamper that day—all but one pair. The only clean pair that I could find, was a pair of Princess Leia undies that my mother mistakenly bought one wretched Christmas.

I sat there, humiliated, as even Timothy Dunkley stood there laughing at me. Timothy Dunkley was no stranger to unfortunate circumstances and accidents, himself, having been ridiculed for years for wetting his pants during a school recital of *A Christmas Carol*. I think I will take my chances with the steps, I thought. I couldn't risk embarrassing myself in front of a girl that I don't even know.

I moved against the wall, as I tiptoed past my mother's room. Everything appeared to be dark and quiet. I softly put my right foot down on the top step, as it let out this loud groan. I sat there for a moment, expecting to hear movement from my mother's room, as I was almost certain she had heard—but nothing.

I proceeded to put my weight down on the second step as it echoed a squeak throughout the silent house. I decided at that point, it would probably be in my best interest to just move swiftly down the remaining steps, since slow and steady, seemed to make more noise than I had anticipated. I walked briskly down the remaining steps as each one seemed to be noisier than the last. I made it to the bottom of the stairs, and looked back up to make sure Mom was still sleeping in her room. I wondered if this was how the prisoners of Alcatraz felt the night they escaped to the sea. The thrill and the rush of knowing that any minute, things can go horribly wrong, and that your perfect plan was not so perfect after all.

I took one last look upstairs, and reflected for a moment on my proud achievement, and then turned to see my mother standing there in front of me.

"What in God's name do you think you are doing?" she said.

I stood there like an escaped prisoner who just made it over the barbed wire fence, only to find himself face to face with the warden.

I thought about telling her the truth—I really did—but I was worried she would call the cops on the poor girl, and my opportunity to make a new friend would be over, before it even began.

"I just came down for a glass of water," I said, as I pretended to clear my throat. "What are you doing up?" I said, acting like I cared.

"I couldn't sleep, so I thought that I would do some reading. Figured it might make me sleepy and I would be able to go back to bed."

"And did it help?"

"Not really. The book was more interesting than I thought, so I just continued reading, and the next thing I knew, it was the middle of the night."

I opened the kitchen cabinet and grabbed a glass that was covered in dust.

"Is there anything in this house that's not smothered in dust," I said, as I carefully rinsed it under the faucet.

"Well, the house has been vacant for six years."

"Yeah, and now I know why," I said, as I tried to think of an excuse to go outside without causing suspicion. I took a mouthful of water, and poured the rest down the drain.

"I think I am going to go outside for some fresh air," I said, as casually as I could.

"At this hour of the night?"

"Yeah, why not? My bedroom is stuffy as hell, and it's hard to get comfortable when you're covered in sweat."

"Well, I think it's an awful idea to go outside. Look how dark it is out there," she said, motioning towards the window. "Need I remind you, that this isn't Scranton, and there are far worse things to worry about in those woods than skunks and raccoons."

God, I hate when Mom comes out with the worst-case scenarios whenever

I did something that was not to her liking.

"I'll be fine; besides, I'll only be gone for a few minutes,"

"Okay, but don't ask me to take you to the hospital if you get attacked by a bear."

"I'm not going to get attacked by a bear, but if by some slight chance I do—I will make sure to drag my bloody body there myself."

"I'm going to bed," she said, as she threw up her hands. She grabbed her book off the table, wrapped her robe around her body, and walked up the steps to her bedroom.

I grabbed my sneakers lying by the door, and walked outside to the front of the house. The chill caused my skin to bump and my body to shiver. The weather has been quite unusual for Maine, with it being unseasonably hot and humid during the day, and colder than normal at night. I should have grabbed a jacket to put over my t-shirt, but with all the commotion, I didn't think to do so. I walk to the back of the house, where I expected to see the girl standing somewhere within the overgrown lawn, but there was no one there. Gradually, and carefully, I made my way through the wild grass and quietly whispered, "Hello?"

I heard nothing but my own breathing. "Are you there?" I called out, as I moved closer to the woods.

Nothing.

Perhaps I dreamt the whole damn thing, I thought, but it seemed too real.

I could still see the girl's image when I closed my eyes, as if it were burned into my retina: Chestnut brown, shoulder length hair, denim jacket, stone wash jeans, and Converse high tops. She had a peculiar beauty about her that made her seem different than other girls that I had previously known. But now she was gone, or quite possibly, just some delusion that I conjured up in my mind. Maybe, subconsciously, I created her, possibly out of loneliness, or some silly attempt at fulfilling some void that is companionship.

I don't know. All I do know is that whoever I saw—whether real or imagined—was beautiful. I like to think, that if in fact, she was some sort of creation from my inner self, that maybe, just maybe, she would come back to visit me one day in my dreams. I walked away disappointed, and confused about the whole situation, but I wasn't going to dwell on it any longer. I will sleep on it, and try to make sense of it in the morning. I walked in to find Mom sitting on the recliner that was still covered in plastic.

"What were you doing out there? I saw you walking in the backyard. Why would you go back there with the grass being as high as it is?"

"Do you miss anything?"

"I see everything. I'm your mother, and that's what good mothers do. Spying, eavesdropping, tapping phones—whatever needs to be done to keep you out of trouble. It's all there in the *"How to Be an Attentive Mother* handbook."

"I'm going to bed—goodnight, Mom."

"Just remember that I'll be watching you."

Yeah--yeah," I said, as I made my way up the stairs.

A few hours later, I awoke to the rumbling drone of a lawnmower outside my bedroom window. I grabbed my swatch off the table and put it on my wrist: 10:20 a.m. "I need coffee," I said to myself, as I let out a yawn. I look out the window to see Mom raging war against the jungle which was our backyard. Crap, she is going to want me to help her, I just know it. I dreaded even the thought of cutting grass, especially a yard such as this, that has somehow managed to be neglected for so many years. Anytime Mom wanted me to cut grass at home, I always used the old allergy trick. I would first agree to do the task, then after about five minutes in, I would start sneezing and coughing. I would then proceed to rub my eyes until they turned red and performed a sort of fake wheezing, that even the Academy would deem Oscar worthy. Eventually, Mom stopped asking, and I would then occupy my day with more exciting things-like playing Nintendo.

I made my way to the kitchen, and dug through the cupboards, in the hope of finding some crystalized coffee, or a teabag—anything with caffeine would do. Nothing here. "Dammit."

Outside, Mom was still occupied with mowing the lawn, and unaware of my presence, as I stood there watching. After about five minutes, she finally noticed me on the back porch and waved. She shut the lawnmower down, and walked towards me while wiping her brow with her hand.

"How long have you been up for?" she said, as she continued to wipe the sweat from her forehead.

"Like 10 minutes. But there is no coffee in the house, and I need coffee," I whined.

"Yeah, I was planning on going to the market to pick up a few odds and ends, I mean, we can't possibly continue to eat fast food every day. Besides, I can use a break from this jungle. Do you want to go for the ride?"

"Nah, just bring back coffee, and maybe some chocolate—I'm dying for chocolate."

"Ok, why don't you finish cutting the grass while I'm at the store." There she goes again with the grass. What does she think? That just because I am in a different state, that my allergies won't be affected. It's not like the grass in Maine is somehow different than the grass in Pennsylvania. I knew it was all one big lie, but give me some credit for trying.

"Mom, you know I would love to, but my allergies can't handle that tall grass," I said, in the most serious tone I could muster.

"Oh, yeah, I forgot about your allergies. Well, you're going to have to start pulling your weight around here. Remember-we are a team now."

"I know, I'll find something to do, but after I have my coffee."

"Okay, I'll be back shortly," she said.

With a slight smirk on my face, I watched her walk away, realizing just how effortlessly lying was for me. I almost started to believe the lie myself, which kind of scared me a bit. I started to walk away, when I noticed a fresh footprint in the mud from last night's rain. I bent down to get a better look and noticed the prints were too small to be mine, and too big to be Mom's.

"Holy moly, hold the guacamole," I said out loud, as I shook my head in disbelief. I can't believe this. So, I'm not losing my mind. I did see the girl standing out here last night. I looked more closely at the ground now, and noticed another footprint, and another, and another—all leading into the woods behind our house.

4. LOOKING FOR A GIRL

I knew in my heart that the footprints belonged to the girl, but the only way to be certain was to follow them. Maybe I could find out where this girl lives, and ask her why she was throwing pebbles at my window in the middle of the night. I was curious about what she wanted, but I also wanted to see her again. I wasn't sure what it was, but there was something incredibly strange and, alluring about her. I ran back into the house and squeezed into an old pair of Levi's and a white t-shirt—just in case I did manage to find this mystery girl. I wouldn't want her first impression of me to be one of disappointment, by showing up in my old sleeping shorts, and a ripped *Pink Floyd* t-shirt.

I needed to make this quick, because if Mom came home to find me not there, she was likely to have a fit. I combed the area for more prints, as I carefully made my way through the thick of the woods. The footprints went on for about another 10 minutes, when suddenly, I spotted movement through the trees. I moved in closer to get a better look, and that's when I saw her. There she was-gracefully swinging on a board attached by two ropes to an old oak tree.

The sun's brilliance was shining down upon her face, and her hair blowing into her eyes as she swung back and forth so elegantly. She looked even more beautiful in the light of day. I approached her quietly, as I attempted not startle her too much by my unannounced presence.

"Hey," I said, "do you remember me? You know—the boy you scared half to death in the middle of the night."

She placed one foot down into the dirt and stopped herself from swinging. She looked at me and smiled. "Hope I didn't frighten you too much," she said, as she jumped off the swing.

"Yeah, it was nothing," I said, trying to play it cool.

"You're lying."

"Okay, the truth is...well, you almost gave me a heart attack."

"A heart attack? I'm sorry about that, it wasn't my intention."

"So, what was your intention?"

"I wanted to see who the new cute boy was that moved into the old Brannigan estate. No one has lived there for years, so obviously, I was a little curious."

I pretended not to notice that she just called me cute, but at that moment, it was all I could think about.

"Our landlord said that it's been abandoned for quite some time."

I was nervously fidgeting with some lint in my pocket.

"My name is Justin by the way—Justin Spencer." I extend my hand as she moved in closer to shake it.

"Nice to meet you, Justin Spencer. I'm Natalie—Natalie Boyer."

"So... What did you want last night, Natalie Boyer?"

"I wanted to welcome you into the neighborhood. It's not every day we get new neighbors, and it doesn't hurt that you are quite the looker, Justin Spencer."

Never had I heard anyone, other than my mother, use the phrase, *quite the looker* when referring to someone's looks. I took notice, but I wasn't about to make a big deal out of it. "Thanks, but I don't think it's ever a good idea to welcome someone to the neighborhood by throwing rocks at their window in the middle of the night."

"Probably not, but that's how we do things in this part of the woods."

"Really?"

"Nah, I'm just messing with you," she said, as she pushed me slightly.

Was she flirting with me, I wondered?

"So, how old are you, Justin Spencer?"

"I'm fifteen, but I'll be sixteen soon."

"Well, that's how birthdays usually go, Justin. You have to turn fifteen before sixteen, and seventeen, and so on, and so on, until one day-pfft."

"So, how old are you?" I asked.

"How old do you think I am?"

"I don't know. I'm not accurate at guessing people' age. I once guessed my friend's mother's age, because she asked me to, but I was way off, and not in a good way."

"C'mon, just take a guess," she said.

"Ok, fine, hmm...seventeen?"

"Close, but no, try again."

"Sixteen?"

"Bingo! I'm just a little older and a little wiser than you, Justin Spencer."

"You know that you can call me Justin, you don't need to use my full name."

"Why, does it bother you?"

"No, it doesn't bother me, but I do find it a bit strange."

"Well, what can I say, I'm a strange girl," she said with a broad smile. "So, what's your middle name, Justin Spencer?"

"Phillip."

I like that: Justin Phillip Spencer. It's a good pen name if you wanted to be a writer."

"I can't write to save my life, but I do love a good book," I said.

Why did I say that, comics don't count as serious reading—do they?

"Really?" she said, "who is your favorite author?"

"Hmm...that is a tough question."

I struggled to think of one serious writer, but my mind did not avail to do so.

"Well, there are so many great writers out there, but, I guess if I had to choose one, it would probably be Smith."

"Smith, huh?" she said, biting her lip. "C'mon Justin, you don't have to lie to me. It doesn't matter if you're not a fan of the literary arts."

"But, I am though, I read all the time."

"What do you read then?" she asked.

"Ok, you got me. I don't read novels or anything, but I do read comics," I said, embarrassed.

"That's cool, what kind of comics?"

"Mostly horror comics. The classics, like the *Wolf-Man*, and *Dracula*."

"Interesting, see, I knew you had some intriguing qualities about you."

"So, I'm assuming you live around here?" I said.

"Yes, you can say that, but stuck would be more like it."

"What about you?" she said. "Where did you live, before coming to our little piece of paradise?"

"Scranton, Pennsylvania."

"Cool, isn't that the city mentioned in that Harry Chapin song?"

I shrugged.

"So, what's the real reason you were throwing rocks at my window last night?" I said. "And don't tell me you just wanted to welcome me into the neighborhood."

"Alright, Justin Spencer, if it's killing you to know. The truth is...I get bored late at night. There is never anyone to talk to, so, I thought I would take my chance with the new boy in town. It just feels like the nights here never end, and the days are reruns of yesterday."

"I feel like I'm never going to be more than what I am right now. Sixteen forever, and stuck in this God-forsaken town."

"Don't say that," I said, "the future is only as big as your dreams, and if you dream big, then anything is possible."

"Ok, Mr. Positive, but you're starting to sound like a graduation commencement speaker."

"Fine, so what is this place?" I said as I pushed the empty swing back and forth.

"This was my playground growing up. My father built this spot for me so I would have somewhere to play and escape reality for a bit."

"Wow, sounds like a cool guy," I said.

"A storm came by a few years ago, and wiped out most of what my father made—except for this old swing."

Natalie lowered her head, and I noticed a sadness about her that I hadn't seen before.

"Are you Ok?" I asked.

"Yeah, I'm fine, it's just that, well, when you're young, there is so much to be optimistic about, but then as you get older, it gets harder to see the positive, or understand why bad things happen to good people. I lost my mother when I was ten to ovarian cancer. I remember coming home from school one day, and my father sitting me down to tell me, that Mom was really sick. I started to cry, but my father reassured me that my mother was strong, and explained to me that I should think positive thoughts, because she was going to beat this thing called cancer. Ten months later, the cancer spread to her ovaries. I remember her lying there in bed, too weak from the chemo to sit up, but somehow finding the strength to hug me. She kissed my forehead, and told me that she would always be watching over me, and that I needed to be strong for my father. Then one day—she died. I remember the funeral, and seeing a frail woman, who looked nothing like my mother, lying there lifeless, in a pearl white coffin, with one red rose in her right hand."

"The image haunted me, and I had nightmares for weeks, then one day—I just didn't think about it anymore."

"I'm sorry for your loss," I said. "I know how it feels to lose someone you love. I lost my father in an automobile accident before I was born. I didn't have that bond of knowing him like you did with your mother, but I think about him all the time, and wonder if he is happy, wherever he is."

"Thanks," she said, as she lifted her head up, and gave me a faint smile.

As much as I wanted to stay there and talk to her, I knew Mom would be upset if she came home to an empty house, when she could use an extra hand with the groceries.

"I'm sorry, but I have to go. My mother has a pretty big list of chores waiting for me, and she will be really mad if I go AWOL on her."

"Go--go, you don't need to explain. I get it," she said, "parents are a drag."

"It was really nice meeting you, Natalie."

"You too, Justin Phillip Spencer," she said, as she sat back down on her swing.

"So, will I see you again?" I asked.

"If you're lucky, you might."

"When?" I said, anxiously waiting her response.

"I'll come to you."

"Ok, just don't come at three in the morning anymore, or my mother will kill the both of us."

"Okay, I promise," she said, "now go home before your mom comes looking for you."

I darted home, out of breath, but just in time to see my mother's car pull into the driveway.

"I need some help over here!" she shouted from the car window.

"I'm coming," I said, still gasping for air, "did you get my coffee?"

"What happened to you?" she said, "it looks like you're going to fall over."

"I'm fine, just out of shape."

"I hope you didn't try cutting that grass with your allergies. I told you not to worry about it."

I wanted to say, yes Mom, I spent the entire time trying ever so diligently to cut the grass, but it overtook me, I'm sorry I didn't get the job done. I wanted the ultimate accolades of praise from my mother, but I just couldn't do it.

"No, I'm just out of breath from running," I said.

"Running? Where were you running? I hope not around the house."

"C'mon, Ma, I think I outgrew that like ten years ago," I said as I rolled my eyes.

"Here, take these into the kitchen," she said, as she handed me two brown bags filled with groceries. I grabbed the two bags, and trying ever so desperately to prove my strength, I went in for a third.

"What are you doing?" she said, "you're going to drop everything all over the place."

"I'm just trying to help."

I settled for the two bags and headed for the kitchen, where I lay them gently onto the counter. I took out each item, and examined it. Detergent, crackers, sugar, bread, cereal, but no coffee.

My mother set down two bags next to mine, and I reached in to examine them.

"Calm down, you're throwing stuff all over the counter, and you're not putting anything away," she said. "Put the stuff you have away first, and then you can help me with these bags."

"Coffee, Mom—I need coffee. Did you get it?"

"Yeah, I got it, just calm down. You're acting like an addict."

"A what?" I said, slightly confused.

"An addict," she said. "The people who need a fix, or a drug to get by."

"Yeah, ok," I said, "compare my need for coffee to a heroin addict; might as well send me to rehab too."

"Maybe I will," she said. She jerked a jar of crystalized coffee out of the bag, and tossed it at me. I clumsily tried grabbing it, as I juggled it in the air for a moment, before catching it between my elbows.

"Are you trying to kill me?" I said. She laughed, but I didn't find it amusing at all.

"So, you didn't tell me where you were running to," she said, as she placed items in the refrigerator.

"I met a friend."

Her eyes widened, and her eyebrows raised, as she gave me this look of astonishment.

"Well, that was quick. What's his name?" she said, still with that goofy smile on her face.

"It's a girl, and her name is, Natalie," I said, as I set a pot on the stovetop to boil water.

"Well--well, my boy has found himself a girlfriend."

"She is not my girlfriend; besides, I hardly know her."

I poured two scoops of coffee into a mug, and continued to wait for the water to boil.

"So where did you meet this Natalie?"

"I met her outside when I was wandering around."

"Oh, does she live around here?"

"I think so, I mean, we really didn't talk long."

"That's great, honey, I'm happy you made a new friend."

"I barely know her, I mean, she seems like a cool girl, but it's too soon to consider her a friend."

"Fine, so when do I get to meet this girl?"

"I don't know; I don't even know when I'm going to see her again. It's not like I was able to give her my phone number, because in case you forgot— we have no phone."

"I'll call the phone company later, but right now, I'm going to finish cutting the grass. Why don't you finish your coffee, and then you can start taking some of that plastic off the furniture?"

"Fine, Ma."

I removed the pot of boiling water from the stove and poured it into my cup. The steam rose as the aroma of coffee permeated the kitchen.

"I'm happy you found someone, sweetie," she said, as her hand caressed my shoulder.

She gave me that look; the look that mothers give you through various stages of your life. I always thought of them as the stages of accomplishments, as we progress from children to adults. They are as follows: Learning to crawl, learning to walk, learning to use the potty, learning to read, and that one thing that just comes naturally; love. It's as if I finally crossed the threshold into adulthood.

"Thanks, just don't make a big deal out of it," I said.

She shot me a smile, and sauntered away to the finish her work in the yard.

I took my coffee into the living room to look over the job that awaited me.

I started peeling back the plastic from the couch, and the chairs, and then proceeded to the coffee table, and the lamps. The furniture was mostly antique items, and they appeared to be in better condition than I had originally thought. Mom loved antiques; me, not so much. They did fit perfectly into the whole theme of the house, and best of all; we didn't need to buy furniture. I looked at my watch: 1:30 p.m. I thought about going outside and letting Mom finish the rest of the cleaning, but once again, my conscience wouldn't allow it. As much as I would have loved to sit there and talk with Natalie for hours, my mom needed me here. I gave myself a small motivational speech, and then cleaned everything that I could.

Dusting, scrubbing, sweeping, mopping, and everything in between; stopping only for the occasional bathroom break, and to eat.

Now, I was no expert on the art of cleaning, and I admit that some of my work was half fast, but I think I did a pretty good job for an amateur.

I looked at my watch: 8:15 p.m. It took me longer than I had hoped, but I was proud of my commitment to get the task accomplished.

"Wow, you really made this place look like a home," Mom said, as she patted me on the back. "I have to admit, I didn't think you had it in you, but here I stand," she said.

"Truth be told," I said, "I wanted to go outside, but I can do that anytime."

"Aww, every day you surprise me with something new. You are a charming young man, and this, Natalie, would be lucky to have you as a friend."

I quickly changed the subject. "So what's on the agenda for tomorrow?"

"I don't know—what would you like to do?"

"Maybe something fun, and a little more exciting than cleaning," I said.

"I agree, let's check out the town tomorrow."

"Okay, but not all day," I said, hoping to see Natalie again.

"Okay, well I'm going to bed," she said.

"Me too," I said, "my body is not used to this much work in one day."

I awoke to the birds chirping, and the lingering smell of fresh cut grass carried by the morning breeze. I looked at my watch. Only 7:38. It took every ounce of my being to drag my fifteen-year-old body out of that bed and into the shower.

Mom was sitting at the kitchen table, reading one of her romance novels by the time I finally made it downstairs.

"I made tea, want some?" she said.

I shook my head, and grabbed the coffee from the cupboard.

"Did you sleep well?" she asked.

"I thought I did, but I still feel like crap, so who knows."

"You're going to have to get used to getting up early again. It won't be long before you will be going back to school."

"C'mon, it's June," I said, "let me enjoy my summer before you go shooting off the *S* word."

"Speaking of school—we will have to get you registered. We don't want to wait until the last minute."

"Are you purposely trying to give me a headache?" I said, "because that's what you are doing. You can't hit me with all this information as soon as I get up—my body isn't prepared for it. It's like attacking a platoon while they're sleeping, or bombing the enemy before breakfast— it's just not acceptable."

"Okay, cranky pants, just drink your coffee, and we can hit the town," she said.

. . .

We arrived in downtown Sherbrook, where some of the finest examples of New England architecture were on full display. Beautiful cobblestone streets were abundant around every corner.

"Pretty awesome, don't you think?" Mom said, while desperately trying to keep her eyes on the road.

"Yeah, it reminds me of the pictures in my history books."

"Look at those houses," she said, "have you ever seen anything so lovely?"

Mom found an ideal parking spot about a block away from the fishing docks and pulled in.

"I have to admit," I said, "the town does have a natural, untouched beauty to it. Something you won't see in Scranton's south side, that's for sure."

"Well, it's a quarter after 10," Mom said, "so do you want to grab something to eat, or see the sights first?"

"You already know what I'm going to say, so why even bother asking me?"

"Out of courtesy," she said grinning, "so breakfast it is."

We ate at a small restaurant called the *Sleepy Lobster,* where a huge lobster was perched on top of a trap above the building. The menu was filled with items that you wouldn't normally associate with lobster. Yes, you had the obvious lobster dishes: lobster bisque, and lobster rolls—but lobster ice cream? Really? Are they trying to make people sick?

I didn't find regular lobster to be appetizing—never mind—lobster ice cream, and lobster pie.

"We should come back here for dinner one day," Mom said, "they have quite the selection of lobster dishes."

"You're on your own for that," I said in disgust.

"Oh yeah, I forgot that you don't eat lobster."

We both ordered the short stack of pancakes, sausage links, and two cups of coffee. Breakfast was enjoyable and the people seemed friendly enough. I might be able to live here after all, I thought.

With our bellies full, and our curiosities leading the way, we made our way through the farmer's market.

"I'm going to see if I can find us some fresh vegetables for dinner," Mom said, "why don't you look around, but stay close-"

I didn't wait for her to finish; my eyes were already fixated on a comic book store across the street.

"MOM!"

I pointed to the store, and she nodded. I made a dash for the store, when out of nowhere, a black *BMW* convertible, full of teen girls, pulled out from a nearby parking lot, nearly striking me. I stood there, visibly shaken in the roadway, as the driver, a Barbie type blonde, laid her hand down on the horn.

"Watch where you're going, dweeb!" she shouted.

The other girls in the car laughed, as they started to drive away, when I noticed Natalie in the back seat. I waved to her with this stupid look on my face, as she laughed and drove away. What the hell? I can't believe she just blew me off like that. Was she that superficial to not even acknowledge me in front of her dimwitted friends? How can she do this to me? I walked away feeling humiliated. I had hoped we could be friends, but after what I just witnessed here—I didn't care if I ever saw her face again.

"I got the vegetables," Mom said as I approached her. "I thought you were going to the comic book store?"

"I don't feel like it; can we just go home now?"

"What's wrong, did they not have what you were looking for?"

"I just want to go, please, trust me on this, Mom, I don't want to talk about it."

She looked disappointed, but nodded and respected my wishes.

The drive home was quiet. Mom knew there was something bothering me, but she gave me my space, which was much appreciated. Natalie didn't seem like the type to be associated with the likes of that crowd, but I suppose my impressions were wrong about her. I was angry with her and just wanted the day to end.

...

I tossed in bed, just staring at my watch, as the minutes rolled by ever so slowly. 12:00 a.m., and here I was, still thinking about Natalie. The night just wouldn't let me go. I only met the girl once, why was I so upset? Maybe it's because she threw pebbles at my bedroom window, as if we were the best of friends, and then had the audacity to treat me as if I didn't matter. I mean, who does that? Natalie Boyer—that's who. God, if I ever see her again—"

Before I could finish my thought, I heard her voice.

5. TWO FACED

"Hey, you awake? It's Natalie—get up, sleepy head."
I jumped out of bed, and made my way to the window, where Natalie was standing below.
"It's not three in the morning, and I didn't use rocks this time," she said, with a grin.
I wanted to curse her out, and tell her what a jerk she was today, but I couldn't. There was something about the way she smiled at me, that instantly made me forget about what she had done.
"You shouldn't be here; my mom is sleeping."
"Yeah, I know. Why don't you come down, so we don't wake her?"
I should have closed the window, and put the covers over my head but I didn't. Instead, I went outside.

The night was brisk, with an October feel to it. I was dressed more appropriately this time around, wearing my Scranton high sweatshirt, and black sweatpants.
"What are you doing here? You really shouldn't be here," I said, trying desperately not to show my anger.
"I know, but I'm bored and nobody else is up."
"It's late," I said, "and I don't think you should be bored at twelve in the morning—you should be asleep at twelve in the morning."
"What can I say, I'm a night person," she said, and then giggled.
I stood there with this shit grin on my face, not able to look her in the eyes.
"What's wrong? You don't seem like yourself," she said.
"I'm fine," I said sarcastically. "What about you? Do you feel like yourself?"
I nervously kicked the dirt, avoiding eye contact.
"You're acting like a jerk," she said.
"Well, maybe this is how people act when they awake to people screaming at their windows at three in the morning."
"First off, it is midnight, and second, I was not screaming."
"Whatever, I don't care for the person I see in front of me. I thought you were one thing, but now I see, my judgment was way off."

"Is that so?" she said.

I stood there silently kicking dirt, and struggling to pretend that it wasn't killing me to ignore her.

"Well...I guess I won't take up any more of your time then," she said. She started to walk away, but I was not about to let her get off that easy.

"My friendship is not something that you can order like a pizza, and then have it delivered whenever it's convenient for you."

"What are you talking about, Justin?"

"You know what I'm talking about, Natalie."

"No, I don't."

"This morning in the convertible with your friends."

"Huh? I still don't have any clue what you are talking about."

"Your friends almost ran me over in their precious little beamer, and you just sat there in the back seat— laughing like a hyena—pretending that you didn't even know who I was. I thought you were different, Natalie, but I was stupid to think that you were any different from any other girl in this shit town."

"Are you high?" she said. "I didn't laugh at you; I wasn't even in town today."

"Oh right, I just imagined the whole incident. Don't patronize me, I know what I saw."

"It wasn't me, I promise you, I would never do that to someone."

"Whatever, I should go—I believe we wasted enough of each other's time— wouldn't you say?"

"I don't know what to say, it wasn't me, Justin, but whoever it was, I'm sorry."

"Goodnight, Natalie, please don't come around again."

I didn't bother looking back as I left her standing there with a staggered look upon her face.

Inside, Mom was lounging on the couch.

"How much did you hear?" I said.

"Well, you weren't exactly quiet about it."

"I'm sorry that I woke you, but I had to end my friendship with Natalie."

"She was out there?"

"Yes, we had an argument, and I told her not to come around anymore."

"Oh, thank God. For a minute, I thought you were talking to yourself. I was afraid you were smoking the hash," she said, as she started to laugh, but quickly stopped, when she noticed that I was not amused.

"I'm not in the mood for your jokes, Mom——this is serious."

"Okay, you're right, I apologize. It's just that, I didn't see her out there. I only saw you."

"She was there; she was just out of your view. It doesn't matter now anyway, because we are through."

"I'm sorry, sweetie, I know you really liked this girl."

"That's my life, Mom. I mean, I always knew I was a loser, but now I'm, just getting the confirmation of what I believed all along."

"She called you a loser?"

"No, not in words, but her actions spoke for themselves. Maybe it would be best for everyone if I just killed myself."

"Stop talking about death, you're fifteen for crying out loud."

"Goodnight, Mom. I had enough excitement for one day."

***

Diary Entry 1. SEPTEMBER 5, 1988

I refuse to start this entry as Dear Diary, just in case I die tragically in a freak accident, and someone discovers this journal—and for the record—this was not my choice. I started a diary, because Mom thought it would be a good idea to write about my feelings, due to all the traumatic events that occurred in my life. I tried explaining to her, that having a diary is strictly a girl's thing, and that the very idea of writing my feelings down in some book, would diminish my masculinity, thus extinguishing any hope of ever having a girlfriend. She gave me two options: write my feelings down, or go to a psychiatrist.

Mom's first choice was to send me to a shrink, but after a few arguments, and the realization that she couldn't afford one, well, this seemed to be the next best thing. So, I gave in. A lot has happened during my summer vacation. Mom found a job working as a waitress at Jimmy's Clams and Yams—a small hole in the wall restaurant in a prime location next to the fishing docks.

The pay was crap, but the food was excellent, and there were always leftovers for her to take home. When Mom received her first paycheck, she surprised me with a black Schwinn, high sierra mountain bike to explore the many trails and pathways surrounding Sherbrook. We took turns doing work around the house, and before long, the place felt like home. We finally have a phone now too, but it would be more useful to me if I had anyone to call.

Things have been going well, and Scranton, and William, were drifting farther away from our memories with each passing day. I still check the old playground for Natalie, from time to time—but so far—no luck. I guess she moved on, and I was trying to do the same. I would still find myself lying in bed some nights, thinking that I heard Natalie's voice calling my name, but by the time I reach the window, all is silent and still.

Perhaps, one day, I'll see her around town and I'll get the chance to apologize, but for now, my focus is starting 10th grade tomorrow at Grentan High school— named after the founding father of Sherbrook: Benjamin Grentan--as if I care. Goodnight diary…

I awoke to the alarm clock piercing my ears, and reminding me, that this was the day I had been dreading for months. Today was the start of my first day at my new high school. I felt a hankering to hit snooze, and roll back over in my bed and sleep, but that was not an option. "I don't want to go," I said out loud, to only myself. Clumsily, I fidgeted with the alarm buttons, and after several failed attempts, the noise ceased.

It's not that I disliked school, the academic part I enjoyed, but the student body on the other hand—now that was a different story. I never spoke to anyone, and they never took notice of me. I would always become the fly on the wall that nobody seemed to notice, and that was perfectly fine by me. It didn't help my popularity any, but it did manage to keep me off the bully hit list. Sometimes, out of sight, out of mind, was all one could hope for in high school. I heard my mom stomping up the steps in a hurry.

"Justin, are you getting up? I made coffee."

"Yeah, I'm up--I'm up," I said, as I stretched my arms, and stumbled to my feet.

"Do you need a ride to school, or are you taking your bike?"

"I'm taking my bike."

"Okay, well, I'm working a double shift tonight, so make sure you are in bed by no later than ten."

"I know," I said.

"Are you nervous about your first day of school?"

"Yeah, I don't really want to go, but, whatever."

"I know," she said, "but maybe this will be different than your last school. Don't forget, you're starting with a clean slate. You can be whoever you want to be, and nobody will ever know the difference."

"Yeah, I guess so," I said.

"Good luck, sweetie, I'm sure you will be fine," she said, as she kissed my forehead, and headed off to fulfill her duties of the day. I, on the other hand, needed coffee if I was going to have any chance of making it through my first day of classes.

The school was about a mile from my home, and on bike, it took me around five minutes to get there. The parking lot was filled with headbangers, next to their muscle cars, and smoking cigarettes before class. When it came to cliques, Grentan High was no different than any other high school in America. The halls were crowded with jocks, cheerleaders, geeks, punks, outcasts, skaters, preps, and stoners—just to name a few. I have yet to have a label attached to my name, and I plan to keep it that way for as long as I can.

I pulled my schedule out of my pocket, and looked to where I had scribbled my locker number in pencil: *Locker 37*. I rushed through the crowd of students gathered outside their classrooms, and found my locker blocked by a couple who were kissing passionately in front of it. "Excuse me," I said.

They moved to the side, while never releasing their lips from one another. I crammed all my books into the small compartment, and pressed on to find my homeroom.

Arriving exactly one minute before class, I found myself in a crowded room with noisy teens—which did nothing to help my anxiety. I headed to a vacant seat in the far-right corner of the classroom and sat down. The laughter and chatter amongst the students made me feel anxious, so I started to draw in my notebook to take my mind off the excessive noise.

"Hello class, I am Mr. Koval, and I will be your homeroom teacher this year." The man looked close to retirement age, with two, long gray hairs, clinging to life on his bald scalp, and saggy skin around his neck, that made me think: gobble-gobble. He wore a burgundy dress-shirt, that was much too tight for his turkey neck, as he dug his fingers around the collar. He spoke in a dry, monotone voice, and emphasized every word at the end of each sentence. I think I might have found the cure for insomnia, and his name is: Walter Koval.

"First, and foremost," Mr. Koval said, "I would like to go around the room and take attendance. So, if you would please bear with me for a moment, and keep your voices down, then this shouldn't take us too long."

Mr. Koval took attendance, and made a few announcements about different programs, and activities going on around the school. I tried to maintain focus, but two girls seated behind me were softly whispering back and forth about some boy named Brad—who may—or may not be cheating on one of them with a girl named Heather. As I sat there, trying desperately to stay awake, a boy with the complexion of white chalk walked in and sat in the empty seat next to me. Mr. Koval raised his head, and with his glasses lowered, said, "And you are?"

"Seth Warner, sir; I'm sorry I'm late, but I had a little trouble finding the class."

"It's understandable," Mr. Koval said. "The first day can be a little confusing, and I'm fully aware of that. Welcome to homeroom, Mr. Warner, and please don't make it a habit of coming in late—and that goes for the rest of you students as well."

I wanted to look over at the boy, whose hair reminded me of Christmas snow, but I didn't want to seem rude. I was being rude though. Why should I be interested in this kid? Was it because he had a different complexion than my own? Of course it was. I dropped my pencil, and as I went to pick it up, I slightly moved my eyes nonchalantly to his face. He noticed my stare, and gave me a slight nod.

"Sorry," I said, feeling terribly embarrassed with myself.

"It's okay," he whispered, and went back to tapping his fingers against the desk.

Class ended, and I pushed my way through the lingering students in the hallway.

"Hey." I looked back to see Seth waving. I paused for a moment, and looked around to see if he was trying to get someone else's attention, other than mine.

"Hey, you," he said again—this time more urgent.

"Me?" I said, with a clueless look on my face.

"Yeah," he motioned, "you left this on the side of your desk." He handed me my history textbook, and attempted to walk away.

"Wait… thanks," I said.

"Sure, no problem."

"I'm sorry if you caught me staring at you in class," I said, "it was incredibly rude of me."

He turned briskly around and looked at me with this deadpan expression. "Yeah, it was rude of you, so don't let it happen again."

I stood there staring at the floor, not knowing what to say in response. Seth then cracked a huge smile and said, "I'm just messing with you, man. You should've seen the look on your face."

I sighed in relief, and laughed nervously.

"I'm an albino," Seth said, "People stare at me all the time, so I'm used to it." He continued, "I thought you actually handled it better than most people—at least you didn't give me the long drawn out stare. You peeked and looked away—not a big deal. And in case you failed to notice, the whole class, including the teacher, was looking at me like I was a sideshow attraction. So don't sweat it."

"Thanks," I said.

"So, what's your name?"

"Justin."

"Well it's nice to meet you, man, I'm Seth," he said, while extending his hand. His handshake was firm.

"Listen," he said, "I have to get to my next class, but maybe I will see you around."

"Yeah, maybe I'll catch you later, Seth," I said, as he walked away.

I made it through my first day without incident, and was headed to my locker, when I saw her. It was Natalie, and she was headed my way.

6. FIRST IMPRESSIONS

Natalie had a different look about her. Different than when I first set eyes on her outside my house over the summer.

She traded in her denim jeans and Converse sneakers, for a more conservative, preppy look. At her side was a tall, handsome boy with a chiseled physique, and a blonde bimbo, wearing a cheerleading outfit. They looked a lot like your typical, high school "IT" crowd, walking down the runway of teenage popularity.

"Hey Natalie," I said, as I waved at her.

She shot me a look, and rolled her eyes, as she went about talking with her friends.

"Bitch," I whispered under my breath, as I slammed my locker. By the time I got outside to retrieve my bike, the sky began to weep and then a heavy downpour swept through the area, and drenched everything in its path.

"Oh, you got to be kidding me," I said as I hopped on my bike. The faster I pedaled, the more the rain seemed to smack my face in opposition. I arrived home after fifteen minutes—soaking wet, and very cold.

The next morning, I awoke to my mother, abruptly shaking me in my bed.

"Wake up—you forgot to set your alarm—it's almost eight!" she yelled.

"Ugh… what?" I said.

"Come on—get up," she said, as she continued to shake me.

"I'm up."

"Come downstairs, I made coffee."

"Ok, just let me take a quick shower first."

"We don't have time," she said, as she yanked the covers off my bed. "You should take a shower before you go to sleep, so we don't have to go through this every morning."

"I know--I know," I said, as I zombied my way out of bed.

A mug of coffee waited for me on the kitchen table. I drank it in a hurry, and hectically ran around the house to get ready for another day of school.

"Hurry up, I need to get to work."

"Go already," I said with a mouth full of toothpaste, "I'll take my bike."

"You don't have time; so, hurry up and I'll take you," she said, throwing a towel at me."

"Fine." I spat out the rest of my toothpaste, did a quick comb over, and out the door we went.

"Just drop me off here," I said, as I pointed to the street one block away from the school.

"What's the matter? Are you embarrassed of your mother? I thought you didn't care about what other people thought of you?"

"I don't," I said, "but I don't need the unwanted attention either. I prefer to stay under the radar—if that's ok with you?"

"Hey, this might surprise you, but your mother used to be a pretty hip chick back in her day. Did you know that I once partied at Woodstock with Canned Heat?"

"Who?" I said.

"Yeah, them too," she said.

"What are you talking about?"

"Never mind, just go to school," she said, as shooed me away.

"Have a nice day, honey." She hard-pressed on the horn several times, before driving away.

Several students passing by diverted their attention towards me and snickered. I pretended not to notice and stared down at the sidewalk. I walked into homeroom five minutes late, where Mr. Koval reminded me that "class starts exactly at eight," and "there are to be no exceptions." What a jerk, I thought. It was only my second day and he was already giving me a hard time.

I walked to my seat in the back and sat down next to Seth. We traded nods trying hard not to stare this time around. Mr. Koval informed the class that we would be watching a video today on the essentials of proper studying, due to last year's decline in academics.

A few students groaned, and several others put their heads down. Seth nonchalantly threw a crumpled note onto my desk. I looked around to make sure no one was watching, and opened it in secrecy under my desk. It read: *Meet me in the cafeteria for lunch, I need to ask you something.* I looked over at Seth, and whispered, "Ok."

***

The cafeteria was filled with rowdy teens eager to talk with their friends during lunch. All the tables were taken by various cliques— with the most popular kids getting the tables closest to the front, and the so-called losers—seated in the back. Seth was already seated in the last of the remaining tables when I tapped him on the shoulder.

"What's up, man?" he said.

"Nothing, what's up with you?"

"Eating lunch, and reading *MAD*." "Sit down, I saved you a seat."

"I'm kind of hungry," I said, "mind if I grab my lunch first?"

"Don't bother," he said, "it's mystery meat on a bun."

"Yummy," I said jokingly, "but nevertheless, I'm starving, so, I think I'll take my chances."

"Okay, suit yourself, but don't say I didn't warn you."

"Okay, I'll be right back."

The lunch line went back about 30 feet, with the cool kids filling their trays first, and the rest of us waiting patiently for them to finish. I felt a tap on my right shoulder, and turned around to see Natalie standing in front of me. I wanted to look away and ignore her, like she had done to me, but that wasn't my style.

"Hey," she said, "do you have a minute to talk?"

"Sure," I said, "it's not like I have anywhere else to be at the moment," gesturing towards the long line of jocks in front of me.

"Listen," she said, "I thought I heard you say something yesterday, and it's been bothering me all night. So, I need to ask you. Did you call me Natalie yesterday when I walked by you in the hall?"

"Yeah, so?" I said sarcastically.

"Why did you call me that?"

I stood there for a moment, completely befuddled over the question she had just asked me, before answering, "Because, it's your name."

"No, my name is Anna, Natalie, is my twin sister."

"Your twin sister?" "Are you kidding me?"

"No, I'm serious, Natalie is my twin."

A million thoughts started to dance around my head, as I tried to make sense of what she was saying.

"Have you seen her?" Anna asked.

"Not since late June," I said. "God, I am such an idiot to have thought you and Natalie were one of the same."

"It doesn't matter," Anna said. "Where did you see her last?"

"She was at my house."

"Your house? Where?"

"Willow Drive," I said, "not far from the playground that your father built."

"She told you about that?"

"Yeah," I said.

"When?"

"I told you-I haven't seen her since June."

"What's your name?" she asked.

"Justin."

"What is your full name?"

"Justin Spencer."

"I need you to listen closely Justin; my sister has been missing since June, and we have no idea where she may be. We have posted pictures around town, organized search parties, and contacted the police, so if you know where she is, then I suggest you tell me now."

"I swear," I said, "I don't know anything. She came around, and we talked like two times, and then I sent her away."

"What do you mean, you sent her away?"

"I thought she was you, and you were her, or whatever."

"What are you talking about?" she said.

"You probably don't remember this, but you and your friends were in a convertible in downtown Sherbrook over the summer, when you nearly ran me over. You and your friends laughed at me, as I stood there like a fool, and when you didn't even acknowledge me, well, I was upset with you-except I was wrong-I thought it was Natalie-but it was you, and you had no idea who I was. God, I feel so bad now for telling your sister to never show her face around my house again."

"And?" she said.

"She never returned. I'm so sorry, Anna, if I had known, I would never have said those things. What do you think happened to her?" I asked.

"We don't know. The only thing we do know, is that she was supposed to meet my father and I for our birthday dinner, but never showed.

"The cops don't suspect any foul play, and seem to think she ran away."

"I didn't want to believe them, but after hearing your story-I'm starting to think that the cops were right all along. Ugh," she said, while gritting her teeth. "How could she be so selfish to put our family through this?"

"What are you doing after school?" she asked.

"Nothing I can think of, why?"

"Would you mind showing me where you live?" I would like to look around."

"Sure, whatever I can do to help."

"Do you drive?" she asked.

"No, I'm only fifteen."

"Do you want a ride home?"

"Sure, if you don't mind," I said.

"Okay," she said, "I'll meet you in the parking lot after school."

"Ok, I'll see you then," I said.

The line was empty now, but I was no longer hungry. I put my empty tray back on the rack, and started to walk out of the cafeteria, when Seth called out, "Hey, where are you going? I thought we had a lunch date?"

"I'm sorry, Seth, I'll have to take a rain check."

"I get it; you don't want to be seen with the weird albino kid." He smirked.

"It's not that," I said.

"Then what is it?" he said. "I see you talking to Anna Boyer, and then suddenly, my company isn't up to par— is that it?"

"No, that's not it," I said. "Wait… you know, Anna Boyer?"

"Know her personally—no—but know of her—yes."

"How?"

"She is only like, the most popular girl in the school. Anna Boyer is dating the star quarterback, Captain of her cheerleading squad, honor student, and a member of every elite group that matters. The question remains: what did she want with you?"

"It's a long story."

"Look at me—does it look like I have anything better to do? I am a solitary enigma, now I ask you, does it get any more pathetic than that?"

Seth wrapped his arm around my shoulders and said, "I have nothing but time, brother."

I exhaled, "Okay, but keep this between us."

After explaining my situation to Seth, and zoning out for the remainder of my classes, I met Anna in the parking lot. She was standing next to her car——a black Cavalier that didn't seem to fit the rest of her flashy persona. "Hey, I was afraid you wouldn't show," she said.

"Why would you think that?"

"I don't know. I feel bad that I bombarded you with all those questions about my sister, when all you wanted to do was eat lunch."

"Don't worry about it. I would be upset too if it were my sister,"

"Do you have a sister?"

"No, I don't, I'm just saying, you know… if I did."

The tall athletic boy that I saw her with on the first day of school walked up behind her, and masked her eyes with his hands. "Guess who?" he said.

"Pete, c'mon," Anna said, "I'm trying to have a conversation here. Pete, this is… I'm sorry, what's your name again?"

"Justin."

"This is, Justin. Justin, this is my boyfriend, Pete."

"Hey, nice to meet you," Pete said. He moved his right hand into mine like he was about to shake it, and then pulled away. "Too slow," he laughed.

How mature, I thought.

"Babe," Pete said, "do you want to go to the mall with me and Jason?"

"I can't," Anna said, "Justin may have some information on my sister's whereabouts."

"Really, is that so?"

"Yeah, so I need to go with him, and see if I can find out anything about Natalie's whereabouts."

"Okay, well good luck, babe, give me a call later when you get a chance."

"Okay," she said.

Pete leaned in and gave her a quick kiss, before zooming off in his red Camaro.

"Okay," Anna said, "so are you ready?"

"Yeah, but are you sure your boyfriend is going to be alright with us spending time together?"

She chuckled. "Who? Pete? He is a puppy dog—and no offense—but you are not my type."

"Of course," I said, "that was stupid of me to think that." Pete knew that he had nothing to worry about. I mean, why should he? He had the body of a Greek God, and I had the body of a geek God.

Anna took a cassette out of her purse and pushed it into her car tape player, as we cruised out of the school parking lot. "Do you like the Bangles?" she asked.

"Not really."

"Are you kidding me? How can you not like them? They are only like, the biggest female group out right now."

"I don't know; I don't really listen to a lot of mainstream pop."

"God, I love them. I saw them twice in concert—once in Portland— and once in Concord."

"Make a right here," I said, pointing to the upcoming street.

"Okay, so how much further?" she asked.

"Just up ahead on your right-the Old Victorian."

"Oh, yeah, I remember this house. Wasn't this place vacant for years?"

"Yeah, but not anymore."

"Obviously," she said with a smile.

We pulled into the driveway, and she put the car in park. We sat there idling for a moment, listening to her Bangles tape, before she killed the engine.

"So, it's just you and your parents that live here?" she asked as we exited the vehicle, and walked up to the house.

"Just Mom and I. My father passed away before I was born."

"I'm sorry. I lost a parent as well. My mother died from cancer when I was only ten."

"Yeah, Natalie, mentioned that to me. I'm sorry."

"So, Natalie, told you about my mother's death, but she failed to mention that she had a twin sister?"

"Yeah, it looks that way."

"It just makes me a little upset, that she didn't even mention me."

"Did she talk about my father at all?"

"Briefly," I said.

"I still can't believe she would do this to us. We have been worried sick

54

about her-not to mention the volunteers who spent hours of their own time looking for her. God, I'm so angry with her right now. My dad is going to be furious when he finds out. Nat has always been Dad's favorite."

"He told you that?" I asked.

"No," she said, "not in words, but his actions spoke the truth. She was Daddy's little girl, and to think she would put him through this. This is going to kill him."

"Maybe you shouldn't say anything," I said, "at least not right away. We don't even know the full story about what really happened-like I said-I haven't seen her in months."

We walked to the back of the house, through the recently cut grass, that looked much different in comparison to where Natalie first stood months ago.

"So, this is where she was?" Anna asked.

"Yeah," I said, "she stood about five feet from where you are standing right now."

"I still don't get it," Anna said. "Why would Natalie throw rocks at your window, if the two of you didn't know each other? It just seems out of character for her."

"Yeah, it was weird," I said. "I was sleeping, and I awoke to her throwing pebbles at my window." I pointed to my bedroom window on the second floor.

"Did she mention why she did that?"

"Her excuse was, she was bored and lonely." I shrugged.

"I don't mean to sound rude," Anna said, "but this whole story sounds kind of... odd."

"No, I swear, it's all true."

"I just can't seem to make sense out of any of this," she said.

"How do you think I feel?" I said. "I told her off, when I should have been angry with you."

"She had the chance to come clean," Anna huffed, "but she didn't-and now here we are."

"So, what now?" I said.

"I don't know. I guess I will go home and break the news to my father, and see what he has to say about all this."

"I'm really sorry about this, Anna; and I wish I had more information to give you, but unfortunately, I don't."

She gave me a skeptical look that made me think that she wasn't sure whether to believe me or not.

"If you see her again, please don't hesitate to call me." She pulled some scrap paper from her purse, jotted down her phone number, and handed it to me.

"Okay, I hope you find her," I said.

"I do too," she said. "I'll see you at school."

***

Mom brought home Chinese takeout for dinner, and after eating and talking about our day for a bit, I felt it was time to tell her all about the situation at school with Natalie's sister, Anna. "Mom, I need to talk to you about-"

A knock on the door interrupted me. Mom furrowed her brow, and hesitated a moment before getting up to answer the door.

"Who can this be? Are you expecting anyone?" she said.

I shook my head. We had been living here for months now, and never had anyone knocked on the front door—rocks at windows, yes, but never a knock on the door.

A female police officer with the Sherbrook Police Department stood outside the door, alongside Anna and a well-dressed middle-aged man with glasses and thick black hair.

"I'm sorry to bother you, Ma'am, but I was wondering if we may have a word with your son." I sat at the table, staring at my untouched eggroll, as I listened carefully to what was being said.

"What's this about, officer?" my mother asked.

"It has to do with the disappearance of a teenage girl who went missing a few months ago. We have reason to believe that your son may have been the last one to speak with her. We just need to ask him a few questions."

Mom shot me a glance before quickly looking back at the cop.

"What? Wait… do we need a lawyer?"

"I really just need to talk to your son, ma'am, and then we can take it from there."

"Justin, get over here—right now."

I could see by the look on my mother's face that she was not happy with me at all. I sheepishly made my way to the front door, where I knew, a series of questions awaited me.

"Justin Spencer?" the cop said.

"Yes," I said while cowering behind my mother.

"This is Mr. Boyer, Natalie's father—and I believe you are already acquainted with Natalie's sister, Anna."

"Where is my daughter? You--You punk," Mr. Boyer, said waving his finger at me, while spewing out obscenities.

"Mr. Boyer," the officer barked, "you are going to have to calm down."

The officer placed her hand between him and I. "Now if we are going to get to the bottom of this, then I'm going to need everyone's full cooperation. Do you mind coming down to the precinct and answering a few questions, Justin-"

Mom quickly interrupted, "Wait a minute—if you want to ask my son any

56

questions, then you ask them here.

"My son did nothing wrong, and you are not going to drag him downtown like he is some common criminal."

"I don't have anything to hide, Mom, I'll go." I stepped in front of Mom and attempted to walk outside, when I felt myself being dragged back in.

"Oh, no you won't—I'm your mother, and you are still a juvenile, and I say, we will talk here."

"That's fine, ma'am," the officer said, "we are just trying to get some answers about Natalie's whereabouts."

Mr. Boyer scoffed, "He is guilty, just look at him, his own mother knows it, that's why she is afraid to let him go down to the station."

"Hey, I'm sorry about your daughter, but I have seen what cops do when they question young naïve children. They walk in innocent, and then they brainwash them into thinking they actually committed a crime."

Mr. Boyer waved his index finger in my mother's face. "So, you admit that it was a crime."

"Oh, give me a break," Mom said, "and get that finger out of my face before I bite it off."

"You're about as sick and twisted as your delinquent son here."

I banged my fist against the door and everyone got quiet. "Listen!" I shouted, "I have nothing to hide, and as much as you all would like to believe that I am some stupid naïve kid—I can assure you—I am not. Now, officer, what do you want to know?"

The officer took statements from Mom and I, and had me take them to the playground where Natalie was last seen. They all seemed to think I was lying about how Natalie came to my window one night and woke me from a sound sleep. Mr. Boyer called me a liar several times during the interrogation, and I felt the others assumed I was, but said nothing. The whole process took over an hour, and by the time I finally sat down to finish my egg-foo-young, I was no longer hungry. It was getting late, and I just wanted to lay in my bed, listen to my Walkman, and let David Bowie sing me to sleep.

"Where do you think you're going?" Mom said, as I attempted to go upstairs.

"To bed—why, is there a problem?"

"Um, yeah. The cops were just here, and you want to go to sleep and forget about it."

"Yes, it's over with, Mom."

"It's not over with. That father seems to think you are involved somehow. I know if that were my daughter, I wouldn't stop until I found out what happened. Now I'm going to ask you a question, and I want you to be completely honest with me. I am not going to be angry with you, Justin, but I need to know the truth. Do you know where this Natalie girl is?"

"C'mon Mom, not you too. I don't know where she is, but I wish I did, because I would let her have it, for bringing this drama into my life."

"Now, if you are done with the questions, then maybe I can get some sleep. Goodnight."

Mom sat there speechless, as I walked away. I knew she wanted to give me hell for talking to her that way, but I guess she figured I had been through enough for one day.

The next morning, I woke with a pounding headache. The night had not been kind to me. I tossed most of the night in bed, for what seemed to be hours, while drifting in and out of consciousness. I did manage to get an hour of solid sleep before the alarm went off. Mom must have still been angry with me about last night, because I smelled no morning coffee brewing. My nose had become accustomed to the aroma of coffee since school started. After a quick stop in the bathroom, I sluggishly made my way down the steps.

Mom was sound asleep on the couch, and still wearing her clothes from the day before.

7. UNDER THE GUN

I quietly made coffee, got dressed, and tiptoed to the door, before letting it slam shut. The morning air was brisk, and I almost considered going back inside to grab a sweatshirt, before deciding against it. As I biked the one mile to Grentan High, I started to think about all the possible scenarios regarding Natalie's disappearance. I wished I never laid eyes on Natalie. It's all her fault that this is happening, and everyone seems to think that I know more than I do. To say that I was worried about Anna, using her popularity to make my life at Grentan High a living hell, was an understatement.

This was exactly the attention that I had tried so hard to avoid, and here I was, my first week at a new high school, and everything was about to come crumbling down upon me.

Today I arrived earlier than usual; the usual crowd of smokers had not arrived yet, and most of the parking lot was still empty. I locked my bike to the rack, and went to the side door. My stomach gurgled, most likely caused by the anxiety that was creeping over my body. I darted to the boys' room, and splashed cold water onto my face. The chill of the running water helped me focus on something other than my anxiety. The beads of water trickled down my face as I stared blankly into the mirror. My reflection, a pale comparison to normal. My eyes like burnt marshmallows from sleepless nights, trying to focus but unable to do so. I shook the water from my hands, but noticed a reflection other than my own standing behind me. I moved to the side, assuming that whoever it was wanted to wash their hands, when I felt a slight push against my back.

I stumbled a bit, and looked to see Anna's boyfriend, Pete, standing there with a wicked sneer on his face.

I knew that the smile was not one of friendship. I had seen this sort of smile before, on my stepfather—it was one of malice.

"I heard the cops paid you and your mom a little visit last night," Pete said, while straightening his already perfect hair in the mirror.

"Yeah, so?" I said while drying my hands.

Pete bashed the paper towel out of my hand. "Mama's boy. I don't know where you're from, and quite frankly— I really don't give a shit. The only thing that I care about, is that my girlfriend's sister is missing, and she seems to think that you know something about it."

"I told the cops everything I know; I swear on my father's grave—I don't know anything else."

"Oh," Pete said, intrigued, "so you're a bastard, as well as a mama's boy?"

I maneuvered around him, but he moved in closer and blocked my exit.

"I need to go."

"You can go," Pete said, "as soon as you tell me where Natalie is." He tugged at the pocket of my t-shirt until it broke free and fell to the floor. I struggled to fight back, but he over-powered me, and threw me to the floor. The door swung opened, and two boys walked in. I attempted to get up, but Pete's sneakers kept my face pressed against the floor. This time I stayed there, afraid to move. I looked to the two boys for help, but got none.

"You're lucky," Pete said, "this isn't over, mama's boy." Pete gave the boys a threatening look, before storming out of the restroom. The two boys giggled a bit, and then carried on with their conversation as if nothing happened.

I arrived late for homeroom once again, and Mr. Koval gave me the usual speech on tardiness, and how tardiness and academic failure are closely related. I must have looked a mess, because most of the class looked at me curiously, as I made my way to the back where Seth was seated. I hadn't even noticed that my shirt was slightly torn in the back, and my hair disheveled until Seth mentioned it as I sat down.

"What happened to you?" he softly whispered.

"A long story, I'll tell you after class."

"Okay," he nodded.

I doodled a bit in my notebook to kill time, and before I knew it, class had ended.

Seth was already waiting in the hall for me when I walked out. "Dude, you look like shit—what happened to you?"

"Pete Tanelli-that's what happened to me."

"Anna's boyfriend?" Seth asked.

"Yeah, that's the jerk."

"What about him?"

"He roughed me up in the bathroom this morning."

"Seriously? What for?"

"Because, he thinks that I'm hiding information about Anna's sister—which I'm not."

"Damn, what a jerk," Seth said, while brushing off some remnants of toilet paper that remained on the back of my shirt.

"Yeah, he is. So, unless you're looking for more unwanted attention, you might want to consider finding yourself a new friend for a while, or at least until this thing blows over with Natalie."

"Who said we are friends?" Seth, shot me a look as serious as cancer, before cracking a huge smile. "Look at me—do you think I give a rat's ass about what people think of me?"

"Thanks, Seth, I don't know what to do."

"I know you probably don't want to hear this, but maybe you should go see Principal Healy."

I shook my head. "I don't think so, the last thing I want to be known as is a snitch."

"Ok," Seth said, "well, when they bury you, I'll make sure the undertaker puts that on your tombstone: Here lies, Justin Spencer, he was a lot of things, but never a snitch."

"Knock it off, nothing is going to happen. Besides, I can handle myself."

Seth pointed to the hole in my tattered shirt. "Well, if you change your mind, and I really think you should, then go talk to Mr. Healy."

"Ok," I said, "I'll talk to you later. I have to get to my next class."

"I'll see you at lunch," he said.

"I don't think so, I'm afraid that Anna will be there."

"Listen to me. You can't hide from this. Hiding only makes you seem guilty, and we both know that you're not—so be there."

"Okay-okay, I'll be there."

The bell rang, and I rushed to the cafeteria to meet Seth for lunch. He was already seated by himself, off in the corner when I approached and sat down next to him.

"So… any problems?" he said.

"No, not since this morning."

"I've been thinking—is there another school around here that I could transfer to?"

"You can't let them win," Seth moaned, "and in case you forgot: YOU DID NOTHING WRONG."

"I know, but this whole thing is getting out of hand- "

Seth motioned for me to look over my shoulder, and there they were: Anna Boyer, Pete Tanelli, and their entourage of teenage clones. I pretended not to notice them, and quickly fixated my eyes back to Seth.

"Are they coming this way?" I asked.

"No," Seth said, "they haven't noticed us yet. It looks like they're talking to their fans first. Is this a cafeteria, or a meet and greet?" Seth joked.

Nervously, I pulled out one of my textbooks, and stared down at it.

"What are you doing?" Seth asked. "Don't tell me you're studying at a time like this?"

"No, but maybe if they see we are busy they won't bother us."

Seth laughed. "I don't think these people would even care if you were on the toilet. They are known for getting whatever they want, and stepping on whoever gets in their way.

"Oh crap," Seth said. "Don't look now, but here they come."

8. HELLO TROUBLE

Anna and Pete sandwiched me in between them, as the rest of their crew scattered like roaches to sit down next to Seth. It was as if the President himself was sitting down for a meeting in the Oval Office, and the Vice President and Speaker of the House were at his side. I looked over at Seth, his head down, pretending to be engrossed in a book about wildlife.

Anna spoke first. "Justin, I know yesterday must have been stressful for you, but how do you think our family feels? We have been stressed out every day since Natalie left us. I, along with my father, and the police, seem to think your story is full of... how do I put this—crap."

"Wait," I said, "I'm telling the-"

"Shut up and let her finish," Pete said, scowling, as he got up in a threatening manner.

I didn't say another word. Pete sat back down and Anna started to speak again.

"I don't want to ruin you, but I will if I have to. My sister—my *twin* sister— means more to me than anyone could ever imagine, and I will stop at nothing, until she is home safe.

"Do you understand that?"

I nodded.

Pete arose from his seat, prodding a plastic lunch spork at my chest.

"She asked you a question—do you understand what she is saying to you?"

I nodded.

Pete cocked his head to the side, and mocked my nod with an impression of someone with a disability. The table erupted in laughter, except for Seth, of course.

"What's that supposed to mean, mama's boy?" Pete snarled as he continued mocking my nod. "I need a yes or a no answer from you."

I wanted to jump across the table and stick that fork up his ass, but I knew better. I was outnumbered, and the truth was—I didn't stand a chance anyway.

Anna looked over at Seth. "Did he tell you anything about my sister?"

Seth fidgeted in his seat nervously, as he looked up from his magazine. "Tell? Who is going to tell me anything? I'm a natural born gossip. People know better not to say anything to me."

Pete grabbed Seth by the shirt, and poked his finger into his chest.

"Listen here you-"

"What is going on here?" Principal Healy, interrupted.

"Nothing," Pete said, "we were just leaving." Anna arose from her seat first, and her entourage soon followed.

"Is everything alright with you boys?" Mr. Healy asked.

I looked over at Seth, and he shook his head.

"Actually, Mr. Healy…"

"Yes, Seth?"

"Justin would like to talk to you in private."

I looked at Seth and said, "What the hell," under my breath.

"Is this true?" Mr. Healy asked. "Do you need to talk to me, Justin?"

"Yes… kind of."

"Okay, why don't you stop by my office at three today—sound good?"

"Yes, thanks, Mr. Healy."

He patted me on the shoulder and went back to making his rounds in the cafeteria.

"Are you crazy?" I said. "They will kill me if they find out about this." I pounded my fist onto the table, drawing some unwanted attention.

"Oh, don't be so dramatic," Seth said, "they aren't going to kill you— beat the hell out of you maybe—but definitely not kill you."

"Oh, this is just great," I said. "I'm going to have to switch schools for sure now."

"Calm down, Mr. Healy is a great principal, he won't let this get out of control."

I put my head down on the table. "I'm done--I'm done," I moaned. "My life is over: fifteen years of trying to fly under the radar, and for what?" I grabbed my book bag from the floor. "I got to go."

"What about lunch?" Seth asked.

"If I'm facing execution, I sure as hell don't want my last meal to be Grentan hot dogs. I need to go and figure this out, I'll talk to you later."

The clock on the wall read quarter to three, and I took a slow walk to Mr. Healy's office. I paced outside the door for several minutes, while debating whether to enter, or just leave. I finally decided to just knock and get the whole thing over with.

"Come in," I heard Mr. Healy say from the other side.

I walked into a large office, with paintings of our Founding Fathers hung about the room. The room smelled of cheap aftershave.

"Take a seat, Mr. Spencer. I understand you have something you want to discuss with me; is that so?"

I looked down at my shoes in the hope of finding some courage there.

"Mr. Spencer, if you don't speak up, then I'm afraid I won't be able to help you. Now what is it that I can do for you today?"

I got up to leave, but Mr. Healy stopped me. "Is this about those kids sitting at your table during lunch? Don't be afraid. Are they threatening you?"

I was going to say no, Mr. Healy, everything is peachy and walk away, but then I thought about how this whole thing was getting out of control, and I could no longer pretend it was going away.

"Yes, but it's more than that," I said.

"Okay, Mr. Spencer," he said as he put a cup of water in front of me. "Let's hear the whole story then, shall we?"

After about an hour of going over the entire story with Principal Healy, and assuring me that he would look into it, I started to make my way outside to retrieve my bike. Anna and Pete were in the parking lot, along with some of the other popularites. Their eyes followed me, as I walked by them to retrieve my bike. That's when I noticed that my tires had been slashed. My heart dropped! I felt like giving up. I wanted to just run away—run back to Scranton, and never look back.

"Looks like you got yourself a flat there," Pete said, as the others looked on. "Did you run over a nail or something?"

"I don't think so," I said, fuming inside.

I unlocked my bike, and walked alongside it, as I pushed on past him.

I could hear the rest of the group giggling, as Pete started to walk alongside me.

"Do you need a ride? That's my truck over there."

"No thanks," I said, as I kept my eyes straight ahead.

"Okay, well, you might want to get those tires fixed. I hate to see you walk all the way home again. "This area can be a pretty dangerous place, despite its friendly appearance. We already have one missing person in this town and we sure don't need another.

"Well, anyway, get those tubes fixed, and, Justin?"

I looked up for a moment.

Pete smiled. "Be careful out there."

Mom was doing yard work out front when I shoved my beaten bike to the ground.

"What happened to your bike?" she said, as she put down her gardening tools and started to walk over.

"Nothing, I don't want to talk about it, if that's alright with you?"

By the look in her eyes I could see she was infuriated.

"This has gone too far," she huffed, "I'm calling your school, and we are going to have a talk with these kids' parents."

"It's not going to work, Mom; everyone thinks I'm guilty. It's gotten so bad, that I had to actually talk to the principal today."

"And… what did he say?"

"He said he would look into it."

"That's it?"

"Yeah, I don't know what to do anymore."

"Well, I'm going down there tomorrow, and I'm going to give those brats a piece of my mind."

"It's not going to help, Mom, if anything, it will only make things worse."

"Then I'm taking you out of that school, it's not safe there. I am not going to let a few punks destroy your education and your future."

"Look at me, Mom—it's not going to work. I know these kids, and they are going to continue to make our lives a living hell, until they find Natalie."

"Well, what are we supposed to do then? Are we supposed to just sit back and pretend that everything will work itself out?"

"No, that's not what I'm saying."

"Then what do you suggest? Because I'm running out of options here. I had to call off work today because my nerves are shot, to the point that I can't hold anything without shaking."

"Listen, I'm going to find Natalie — I won't stop until I do."

"That's a great idea, honey, but I'm afraid it's not that simple. If the cops can't locate her, then what chance do you have."

"I don't know, but I'm going to find her… I have to."

Mom and I had a quiet spaghetti dinner, and after, I went to my room to think. There must be a way to find out what happened, but where do I look? *Where would a detective start his investigation,* I wondered. Although, I did own a few Dick Tracy comics, I doubt they would do me any good in this particular situation. I guess we can start where any good investigation starts—from the beginning—the scene of the crime if you will.

My thoughts were soon interrupted by the phone ringing in the distance, and a few seconds later, I was requested downstairs.

"Who is it?" I asked, as Mom handed me the phone.

"Somebody named Seth?"

I nodded and shooed her away for some privacy. We had one phone in the house, so I felt that on that rare occasion when I did receive a call, it was only common courtesy to allow me a little privacy.

"Seth?"

"Yeah."

"How are you holding up?"

"Not that great, but whatever."

"Are you going to be at school tomorrow?"

"Yeah. Why?"

"Because I need to talk to you."

"Just tell me now, Seth, don't keep me guessing."

"I don't think so."

"Why not?"

"Because, I'd rather talk to you in person about it."

"Okay, well I'll see you tomorrow then."

"Okay, man, I'll talk to you later."

I hung up the phone and peeked into the living room, where I could see my mother's eyes overlooking her novel. She quickly went back to her book when she noticed me, and I just shook my head.

"So, what was that about?" she asked, her eyes still focused on her book.

"I'm not sure; I guess I'll find out tomorrow."

"Who is this Seth? You never mentioned a Seth."

"Just some kid I met in school, but with everything else that has been going on, I guess I failed to mention it."

She looked up from her book. "So, he is your friend?"

"Yeah, I guess you can say that."

"So, you trust him?"

"Yeah, I do. I know I've been let down so many times before, but he might be the only person in the whole world that gets me."

Mom cleared her throat. "I think you're forgetting someone else."

"C'mon Ma, that goes without saying."

"Well, I think we had enough excitement for one day," Mom said.

"I'm going to read a few more pages of my novel, and then I'm going to try and get some sleep. I will see what I can do about your tires tomorrow."

"Okay, goodnight, Mom, and thanks."

"Goodnight," she said.

I decided to set my alarm clock for 3:30 in the morning so I could get a head start on my investigation. At that moment, I was done doing nothing. If the cops and Natalie's family wanted to focus their attention on me then I would need to start doing my own investigation.

I awoke several minutes before the alarm went off, and gathered my belongings for a chilly night out in the woods. Jacket, sneakers, flashlight, Swiss Army knife, and my REO *Speedwagon* cap. Mom was fast asleep and snoring away, as I made my way past her room. The floors made their usual creaks and groans as I tiptoed down the stairs undetected. I walked outside to the yard, where no moon was visible to offer any guiding light, so I turned on the flashlight and aimed it towards the woods. There was some rustling coming from the bushes and I decided to move in closer to investigate.

Little by little, I made my way to where the sound emanated. My hands trembled with fear and the flashlight shook as I tried to keep it steady. The sound was louder now, and the movement seemed more panicky, as something scurried through the bushes.

I steadied the flashlight on the movement but it was too fast. I moved in closer and listened carefully. The air grew silent, my body still trembling, my heart pounding like a wild drummer. I reached into my pocket and dug out my Swiss Army knife as I attempted to enter the woods.

My senses were on full alert. Flashlight, and knife in hand, as my body prepared itself for attack mode. Whatever it was, I was ready for it. I walked about two feet from the bushes and something moved from within. I pointed the light at the spot and ran in screaming.

I raised my tiny blade like a knight going into battle and yelled out *"Carpe Diem!"* as I made my ambush on the moving object. I leapt forward like a superhero in one of my comics, and stuck the knife repeatedly into the bushes. I heard a loud yelp as blood squirted out onto my shirt. I stabbed the bushes wildly, continuing, until everything went silent. I stood up and dusted myself off, as I looked down to see a dead opossum with my knife stuck in its side.

"Oh my God, what have I done?"

I'd never killed so much as an ant and now this innocent creature, probably just looking for food was dead because of me. I left the knife sticking out of the rodent—too frightened to retrieve it and bear witness to any more carnage that I'd caused. I grabbed my flashlight off the ground as I continued toward the playground.

The playground had an eerie silence to it, as the swing moved slowly back and forth. The fog surrounding the old oak was as thick as pea soup and I waved my hands carelessly in front of me to prevent myself from hitting anything.

9. TAKING A STAND

"Natalie?" I said half-heartedly, as I made my way around the mist. The grass was overgrown and I nearly tripped over a rock hidden underneath its camouflage. I looked down to see a stone with something engraved into it. I dusted off the rock with my sleeve, and shined my flashlight onto the words: *To My Dearest Natalie, The World Is Your playground, Love Father.*

A pile of boards stacked up against the side of a nearby tree caught my attention, as I walked over for a better look. I tossed the dry rotted boards to the side, and uncovered what appeared to be the remnants of an old sliding board. Time had taken its toll on this place, but I imagined that Natalie spent most of her youth enjoying this playground in its prime. It's a shame that it had been forgotten the way it had.

"Natalie?" I said, but this time more urgently.

"So, the Prodigal Son returns," she said.

I spun around and there she was. It was Natalie: the girl that everyone was so desperate to find, and there she was, standing before me.

"Natalie, where have you been? Your family is worried sick about you—not to mention the great deal of stress that you managed to bring into my life."

"You told me to go away, and to never bother you again, so that's what I did."

"I know what I said, but I said it under the assumption that you where being a bitch, when in fact, it was your sister who was the bitch."

"Huh?" she said, as she tilted her head to the side.

"Never mind. This whole thing could have been avoided if you would have just told me from the beginning that you had a twin sister. You made a fool out of me, Natalie."

"I'm sorry, but you don't understand, Justin-"

I quickly interrupted. "I do understand; I understand that you were only thinking of yourself. I understand, that you had no intentions of being my friend, and I understand, you are a selfish little brat who thinks that everyone should just drop everything and cater to you. That's not how life works, Natalie."

She turned and started to walk away.

"Where do you think you're going? Are you going to run away again? Well go ahead, run away, Natalie, it's the only thing you're good at. Who cares if your family is worried sick, or that I'm under investigation for your disappearance."

She looked at me expressionless, before sitting down on the swing and staring at the ground.

"Come on, we need to go," I said. "I need to get you back to your family."

"I can't," she said, "you don't understand."

"Why--Why can't you go back? And what makes you think that I won't drag you from that swing, and bring you back myself?"

"You can't do that," she said.

"Why?"

"What are your religious beliefs?"

"That's kind of a strange question to ask, don't you think?"

"Please, just answer the question."

"Fine, I was raised Catholic, but I don't really follow any religion anymore. Now can we get going?"

"Do you believe in life after death?"

"I don't know—I guess so," I said. "I like to believe that there is more to death than just being maggot food, but that's a topic for Sunday school, or church. Why are you asking me all this?"

"There is a reason for all of this," she said, "but I need you to have an open mind."

"My mind is open," I said, "now tell me already, because you're starting to freak me out."

"The reason why I can't go home, and nobody knows where I am, is because… I'm dead."

10. A DEAD GIRL SPEAKS

"Regardless of what you did, or think you did," I said, "the fact remains-your family just wants you home. They don't want you dead, and I doubt that you will even be grounded - even though I believe you should for causing all this trouble."

"No," Natalie said, "you need to listen to what I am telling you.

"Look at me, Justin, do you notice anything odd about me?"

She befuddled me with the question. "I don't understand what you're trying to tell me."

"You're not listening—look at my clothes—haven't you noticed they haven't changed since that night I came to your window?"

"Yeah. So, you like to wear the same clothes on occasion—who cares? Occasionally, I've been known to wear my *Violent Femmes* t-shirt for three straight days, and nobody ever gives me any shit about it."

"I don't expect you to understand, Justin, but you need to listen."

"Okay, I'm listening."

"I'm dead, and for some unknown reason, only you can see me. I was by your house the day you moved in, and you briefly glanced over at me, before walking away. It was the first time that someone acknowledged my presence. Do you remember?"

I tried to wrap my mind around what she was telling me, but the whole thing sounded insane.

"This is crazy. I don't know whether to call the police, or have you committed to the psychiatric unit."

"I'm not crazy, and neither are you, but I need your help."

"You don't need my help; you need a good psychiatrist."

"Enough with the jokes," she said, "please, I'm begging you… you are my only hope."

There was something desperate in her eyes, that made me want to forget everything I knew about logic and reasoning, and toss it out the window. In that moment, I wanted to believe everything she was telling me, but what would that make me? "Okay, Natalie, I'll humor you for a bit. So, let's say hypothetically, that everything you are saying to me is true—what can I possibly do to help?"

"I need you to find out who murdered me."

"Murdered you? Ok, this has gone too far, Natalie—you need to go home."

"I can't. Are you not listening? I'm stuck here. You need to find out who murdered me—it's the only way I can move on to the next life."

"Okay," I said, "if you don't want to go home, then I can't make you, but, I'm going to call your sister and the cops, and let them know that you are safe. I really hope that you contact them, because everyone is worried sick about you."

"Would you please shut up and just listen to me?" she screamed. "I can't do anything, because you are the only one who can see me."

"Believe me, I have tried, but nobody can see me, except you."

She grabbed my arm in one last desperate plea. Her touch as cold as morning snow, as I pushed it away.

"Please, that's enough, Natalie," I said, "now this has gone too far. I don't know what kind of drugs you are on that are causing these delusions, but please, I am begging you, get some help before it's too late."

I started to walk away, but Natalie tugged at my sweatshirt and started to speak.

"Your father: He was tall, around six foot two, dirty blonde hair, and an athletic build. He had a kind smile, to match his gentle soul. He met your mother while they were both freshmen in college. He eventually had to drop out of school to take care of his ailing father, and took a job at a manufacturing warehouse. His hands were big, and callused from working in the factory, but he enjoyed getting his hands dirty. He worked as a mechanic during his spare time, so that he would have extra money for when you were born. He was working late the night that he was killed by a drunk driver who swerved into his lane. He was able to move on from this life, because it was his time. He knew that his legacy would live on through you—his son."

If I had a mirror to look back at my reflection, I doubt I would recognize the person who was staring back at me. I could feel the color drain from my face, as I stood there listening to the vivid details about my father, that no one, other than Mom, might have known. My legs started to shake, as if a tremor was occurring underneath my feet. I grabbed hold of Natalie for support, but quickly fell through her, and hit the ground. My body felt like it was being pierced with needles and pins, as I reached for a branch and pushed myself up.

"I don't--I don't understand," I said, as I put my hands over my face, attempting to hide the reality that was unfolding before me. I wanted to pinch myself, and tell myself to wake up, but I knew this was no dream. A breeze chilled my nose, reminding me, that this was all too real to dismiss.

"How do you know those things about my father?"

"I told you—I'm dead. I can't reach out and physically see, or communicate with your father, as he is now, but I can see his former self. It's one of the perks that I acquired, while being stuck between two worlds."

"I need to think for a moment," I said.

My body felt as empty as a church on Monday morning, and I started to wobble, before managing to perch myself against a tree for some balance.

"I don't want to scare you," she said, "but I don't have anyone else to turn to. I don't want to be stuck in these woods forever."

"Do you think there is something within these woods that is keeping you here?" I asked.

"I don't know. The only thing that I could think of that made any sense to me—was that maybe—it was because this place was special to me as a child."

"I still don't know how I'm going to help you move on. You say you were murdered, but how do you know?"

"It is a sense of dread that I feel: an overpowering void of darkness and hate, that surrounds my soul, caused by those responsible for my murder. But I need to find out why I was murdered, and who did this to me. I need your help, Justin… I need to be with my mother."

The sadness in her voice tugged at my heart, and either she was crazy, or I was for enabling the idea, but I started to believe her. There was no denying that I saw myself fall through her, and the pain in my ankle reminded me of that.

"Okay," I said, "I will help you. I don't know how, but we will figure this out together."

I left Natalie before Sunrise, promising her that I would return later that night. Mom was sleeping soundly in her bed by the time I got home. I discreetly made my way around the house, while going through my normal school day routine. I was exhausted, but I knew that I had to make it in today, so I could find out what Seth wanted to talk to me about. It had to be something important if he couldn't discuss it over the phone. I drank the last of my coffee and started to rinse my mug out, when I saw Mom walking towards me in her long pink bathrobe.

"Good morning," she said, "I thought I smelled coffee."

"Good morning, Mom, how did you sleep?"

"I slept peaceful," she said, as she grabbed a mug and filled it with coffee. "I don't remember the last time I slept like that. I'm sorry I woke up so late, sweetie, but give me a minute to finish my coffee, and I'll give you a ride to school."

"It's okay," I said, "I don't mind walking."

"Nonsense," she said, "just give me a minute to finish my coffee—which reminds me—I have to stop by the bicycle shop before work to buy you some new tubes."

"Ok, thanks, I'll be outside waiting in the car."

Mom dropped me off at my usual spot, a block away from the school. She didn't blow the horn this time, and I appreciated the gesture. I made it to my homeroom unnoticed, and found myself unusually early for once. Most of the student body were talking amongst themselves, or half asleep, as I went to the back. Seth, already seated in his usual spot, had an uneasy look on his face.

"Hey, Seth. Is everything alright?"

"Yeah, man, I'm ok, but I'm more concerned about you."

"What do you mean?" I said, as I tossed my bookbag off my shoulder and onto the floor.

"Yesterday, after lunch, I started to feel sick from eating three servings of the mystery meat special. So... I went to the boy's room, where I locked myself in the stall and was about to--"

I quickly interrupted him. "I don't need to know the gritty details, Seth - just tell me what happened."

"Ok, so, I was in the stall doing," he paused for a moment and looked around before he continued, "my business, when suddenly, I heard two voices. I recognized the one voice to be, Pete Tanelli, and he was talking to someone else, but I couldn't quite make out who. So, I put my feet up to make it look like the bathroom was empty, and I overheard them talking about you."

"Me?" I said. "What did they say?"

"From what I could make out, it looks as though they are planning something against you this weekend.   "It doesn't sound good, Justin. You might want to consider keeping a low profile for a while. Do you have any close relatives that might be willing to let you hide out for a few months?"

"Are you crazy? I'm not hiding out for a few months over some high school B.S. Besides, I have nowhere to go."

"Well you have to go somewhere, you can't stay here, or they are going to come for you."

"What would you have me do, Seth? Should I join the witness protection program?"

"I don't know," Seth said, "but this whole thing has gotten me perturbed, to the point that I don't think we should be seen with one

74

another for a while."

"What?" I said, "are you serious?"

"I'm not saying forever, just until this whole thing blows over."

I grabbed my bookbag, and rose from my desk. "You know what, Seth."

He looked down at his book, too ashamed to make eye contact.

"Out of all the kids in this school," I said, "you appeared to be one of the few, who couldn't care less about what people thought of you. I liked that about you, and now you just want to run away, because you fear some high school delinquents."

"C'mon, man, it's not like that at all," he said, as he looked at me with those piercing blue eyes.

"Good luck, Seth, and thanks for being my friend for a few days—it's been a real pleasure."

I started to leave, but Mr. Koval blocked my path, holding out a long measuring stick in front of my body.

"Where do you think you're going, young man?" Mr. Koval said.

"I'm leaving."

"I'm afraid you're not. You see, in my class, you need permission and a hall pass to be excused. Is that understood, Mr. Spencer?"

I was in no mood to deal with Mr. Koval, and I was not about to give in and sit back down next to Seth.

"Why don't you take that ruler, attach it to the hall pass, and shove it up your ass: I'm out of here."

The class broke out in a roar of laughter, as I knocked the ruler out of his hand and onto the floor. His face turned sauce red, as he clenched his fist and attempted to take a swing at me. I don't know if he was trying to scare me, or if he was just that bad, but he missed my face by a mile.

"You get back here, Mr. Spencer!" he shouted.

I slammed the door behind me, and ran through the halls, where I made my escape to the school parking lot.

I ran all the way home without stopping for so much as a breather. I walked into the house, out of breath, and dripping sweat, as I grabbed the telephone receiver, and pressed it against my ear. I didn't want any more trouble from Natalie's family or friends, and I just wanted my life to go back to normal. I had the desire to call the cops, and tell them about what really happened to Natalie. I wanted to tell them that she hadn't run away from home, and that she would never return home, because someone murdered her. I was desperate to scream into the receiver to anyone who would listen, and say- "*there is a murderer on the loose in the town of Sherbrook, and they killed, Natalie Boyer.*" I wanted to say a lot of things, but I was afraid they would take me for mad, so, I said nothing at all.

It all sort of sounded deranged, when I replayed the whole scenario out in my mind. I don't know what is real anymore, I thought, as I hung up the phone. I suddenly recalled Amelia, and the brief conversation we had at the motel, about the special gift that I possessed. Amelia would have the answers that I sought, and even if she didn't, it still would be nice to talk to someone who didn't think all of this was foolish.

***

It took longer than I expected on foot to reach the Leisure Inn where Amelia had been staying. I was exhausted, but I managed to dawdle my way over to room 21, and knock on the door. I heard footsteps approaching from within, and the door slowly unlatching its locks. The door opened, and there stood Amelia, smoking her usual clove cigarette, and wearing an outfit that looked like it belonged in a 1960's thrift shop display window.

"Justin," she said smiling, "it's so nice to see you again. Won't you come in? I have some tea brewing if you would like a cup?"

"No thanks," I said.

"Here," she pointed to the couch, "sit down. So, to what do I owe the pleasure of this visit," she said, as she made herself comfortable in her recliner.

"I don't know how to say this, so… I'm just going to come right out with it."

"Go on, dear, I didn't think you'd come all this way to have tea with an old woman."

"Do you remember that first day I bumped into you, while I was searching for the ice machine?"

"Yes."

"Well… you mentioned something about a gift, and…I…umm— "

"And you want to know what I meant by that?" Amelia said.

"Yes."

"Okay, so I am guessing that since you are here, something must have changed your mind about all this?" She took a long drag off her cigarette and exhaled up towards the ceiling. "Because, correct me if I'm wrong, but the last time I mentioned it, you took me for a witch."

"Yeah, and I'm sorry about that."

"It's ok," she said, "I shouldn't have just blurted it out that way. I've never been much of a storyteller, I'm afraid. I always get right to the end, and skip all the chapters in between. Anyway, I believe you had a reason to come here, so let's not delay any further, shall we?"

"Do you want the short version, or the long?" I said.

"Well, if it's going to be the long version, then I suggest, I make you that tea after all."

I told her everything-from the nightmare I had at the motel, to Natalie contacting me from beyond the grave. She listened without flinching, or raising an eyebrow. When it was all over, she took a sip of her tea, and took my hand in hers.

Her voice was soft and serious: "You need to help this girl move on, Justin. She has come to you, because you are the only one who can see her, and without your help, she will disappear from this world, without finding the closure she needs to make the journey into the beyond."

"So, you believe me then?" I said. "You don't think I'm going crazy?"

"Sometimes the people we think to be insane, or delirious, are quite the opposite. When you observe, someone mumbling to themselves on the street corner—do you think they are sane?"

"Not necessarily," I said.

"Just as no one can hear your conversation with Natalie, the person on the street, who you believe to be talking to themselves, could quite possibly be communicating with an unseen entity."

"So, you're telling me that everyone that I have ever seen talking to themselves, has the gift of communicating with the dead?"

"I didn't say that. I said, sometimes that may be the case."

"What about the others?" I asked.

"Crazy, most likely, but regardless- don't ever judge someone because they don't fit your definition of what it means to be normal."

"What do I do now?" I asked, "I feel like I'm alone in all of this."

"You are going to help find that girl's killer, so her soul can move on."

"Move on where exactly?"

"Nobody really knows, and everyone that does know, is dead.

"Some call it Heaven, or Nirvana, but that is what we are accustomed to— mostly from our teachings and literature. All I know, is that this girl is deceased, and she should not be here amongst the living. We must help her find her way to the other side."

"I don't know where to start," I said. "Everyone thinks that I had something to do with her disappearance, since I was the last one to see her."

"You can't go to the police," she said, "they will automatically assume that you are involved in the murder."

"But, I didn't do anything," I said.

"I know that, and you know that, but the police don't know that. The police are only going to see a boy, claiming that Natalie was murdered, because that's what her spirit relayed to you. Remember how crazy I seemed to you when you first met me?"

I nodded.

"Well, that's the way the cops are going to be looking at you, if you go in there with stories about a ghost.

"No," she said, "if you are going to help this girl—then you are going to have to do it without the help of the police. You mentioned earlier that you believe she is trapped within the boundaries of the Playground, and the surrounding woods?"

"Yeah, at least that's what it looks like."

"Then there must be something that is keeping her at that location," she said. "You need to look around, and search for any clues that might help. If you make contact with her again, then talk to her, and ask her what she remembers about her last night alive."

"I thought you said this was a gift, Amelia? The whole thing seems more of a curse than anything else."

"No, don't ever think that way, Justin. This is a gift, and though it may not seem like one at this moment—it will uncover its truth to you when the time is right."

"I just don't understand why it has to be me. I'm fifteen years old for crying out loud. I shouldn't be worried about solving a murder, or socializing with a dead girl. I just want to be a normal teenager, with normal problems. I want to go to the prom, find love, lose love, get acne, and complain about my mom to my friends—I just want things to be normal."

"Unfortunately," she said, "normal will never be in your vocabulary. You can choose to ignore this gift if you must, but you were chosen by some greater power, to help those who can't help themselves."

"Yeah, I suppose you're right, but it still sucks. Do you mind if I call you for advice, Amelia?"

"I don't own a phone, but you are always welcome to visit me anytime you'd like."

"Ok, thanks a lot for the talk," I said, "I do feel a little better."

"You're welcome, dear, and please be careful. If what Natalie told you was true, and she was murdered—then chances are, her murderer is going to do whatever it takes to keep the truth buried—even if it means killing again. Keep your eyes open, and your ears in tune."

"Thanks," I said, "as if I didn't have enough to worry about the way it is."

"You'll be fine," she said.

***

I made my way home around 6:30, and found my mother's car already parked out in the driveway. As I walked up the steps of the front porch, my body became tense and rigid, as if it were shutting down out of fear. An uneasy feeling made its way into the pits of my stomach, as I opened the door to see my mother lying on the couch. I closed the door behind me and walked into the kitchen without saying a word.

"So, how was school today?" Mom said in a calm voice.

I knew something wasn't right, and I was preparing myself for the worst. I thought about lying, which is probably what I would have done, if I believed for the slightest second, that I could get away with it, but, I decided it was in my best interest to be honest and tell her the truth.

"I left school early today," I said, as I waited anxiously for her response.

"And, why did you leave school early?" she asked.

Her voice was tenser this time, and I knew the thunderclouds were moving in before the storm.

"I...uh..." I stumbled for the right words to say, but there was no use—I was doomed.

"You what?" she said, as she got up from the couch.

"I... um... I had a problem."

"Oh, so you had a problem?" she said. "That's funny, because the last time I checked, telling a teacher to shove something up his you-know-where, was not a problem—it's only a problem for the student, who stupidly said the comment in the first place."

"Listen," I said, "it's not what you think, that teacher was-"

"Enough, Justin," she said, "I don't know what's going on with you anymore. I was praying that this move was the right decision for us, but now I am starting to question everything. Since we have been here, it has been one thing after another with you. What is going on in that head of yours? Maybe we should just move back to Scranton, at least William seemed to keep you in line."

"How dare you say that," I said, scowling, "you want to know why I am so messed up, Mom? It's because of you. I'm glad Dad is dead, because I would hate to have him see how screwed up our lives are because of you."

Her eyes started to swell, as she raised her hand back in an attempt to slap my face. I grabbed her wrist, and she screamed, before falling to her knees and sobbing uncontrollably. I snatched my jacket from the coat rack and made a dash for the door, slamming it behind me.

I wandered around town aimlessly for hours until my feet grew tired and sore. It was late, and I knew that whatever hell awaited me at home, was not going to just go away. I thought about running away, but I had nowhere to go, and not to mention, no money. My stomach was hollow and gurgled for something to eat. The only food that I had put in my belly all day was some butter cookies and tea; compliments of Amelia. I had no choice but to go home and face the consequences of my actions—the only question is: does Mom want me there?

The house was dark, with no sign of light, or movement from within. I thought about going to the playground to look for Natalie, but I was too upset. I just wanted to get inside, grab something to eat, and go to bed. I didn't want anything to do with the paranormal tonight. I walked to the kitchen, where I made myself a peanut butter sandwich, and poured myself a tall glass of milk. I ate in a hurry and treaded lightly up the steps, but there was no way around the racket of the wood under the pressure of moving feet. The sound of my mother's bed springs let out a high-pitched squeak, as she changed sleeping positions. If she did hear me come in—she didn't say anything. I set my alarm for school, and fell asleep within minutes.

I awoke much like any other morning, the alarm emitting its annoying beep, and the aroma of coffee lingering throughout the house. I dreaded going downstairs and facing the inevitable fate of last night's actions, but after several minutes, I found the courage to do so.

Mom, was talking to someone on the phone, as I grabbed a cup from the cupboard and tried to act like nothing had happened. When she saw me, she thanked the person on the other line and hung up.

"Sit down," she said.

"Mind if I get my coffee first?"

"You can have your coffee when I'm finished speaking."

"Fine," I said, as I slammed my empty mug down on the table, "let's get this over with."

"Don't give me that attitude," Mom said, her nostrils flaring. "I am trying my best to have some patience with you, so please, enough already." Anytime Mom was angry, but trying to hide it, she had this habit of moving her hands when she talked. I guess it helped distract her, when all she really wanted to do was scream at me.

"Okay, I'm sorry," I said, "now what do you want to talk to me about?"

"Justin, that was your principal on the phone. We had a long talk, and we both feel that it would be best if you didn't go back to school for a while."

I jumped up out of my seat. "No, you can't decide my life for me— I'm going to school, whether you like it, or not."

"You are not going to school," she said, "now that's final."

"Want to bet?" I started to walk away. "Just watch me."

"You can't go back there—you've been suspended."

"Suspended?"

"Yes, I am sorry, but, if you go near the school, they will have you arrested."

"Suspended?" I said, as I sat down.

"I think this could be a blessing in disguise," she said. She attempted to comfort me, by putting her hand on my shoulder, but it wasn't working.

"How is this a blessing, Mom? I've been suspended from a school, where I've been a student for less than a week. I mean, that has got to be some sort of record."

"Well, between those bullies who slashed your tires, and those idiots who seem to be convinced that you know where that missing girl is—this is a blessing. You just need some 'you' time. I will give you your space, and when things start to get back to normal around here, then maybe we can consider another school."

"I don't want to go to another school. I'm sick of running away from my problems. Look what happened—we ran from Scranton to escape our problems there, and we run into new problems here in Maine. The problems will follow us wherever we go."

"I know," she said, "but this time we really don't have a choice."

"So, what's going to happen exactly?"

"Principal Healy explained to me that you will be suspended for a month, and after that, the school board would vote on whether you should be allowed to return after your suspension."

"Oh, that's great," I said, "what am I supposed to do for an entire month?"

"I don't know, maybe get some work done around here, or ride your bike. You're a smart kid, I am sure you will think of something to occupy your mind. Meanwhile, I suggest writing an apology letter to your teacher, Mr. Koval, and to Principal Healy. It can only help your case."

"So… what about us?" I said, "are we good?"

"Yeah, we're good, besides, you are my son, and I'm not allowed to stay mad at you. Now go have your damn coffee," she said with smirk.

"Did I just hear you curse?" I said.

She put her index finger in front of her mouth, "Shh," she said, as she walked away.

Later in the evening, I decided to write the apology letter. I wanted to justify my behavior in the letter by explaining why I did what I did, but I knew that's not what they wanted to hear. They wanted to hear how sorry I was for being an unruly student, and for letting my emotions get carried away by teenage angst. So, I fed them the crap they so desperately yearned for. I wrote my letter as follows.

Dear Mr. Koval, and Principal Healy,
I am writing to apologize for my selfish actions during homeroom, on the morning of September 8, 1988. What I said, and how I behaved, was juvenile, and disrespectful. I am sorry if my attitude has caused you stress in any way, and I was not raised to behave in such a manner. I hope that you can both find it in your heart to forgive me, and I truly am sorry, and embarrassed by my actions.

Thank you
Justin P. Spencer

It killed me to write such hogwash, but I knew it had to be done, if there was going to be any chance of me returning to school after my suspension. Who knows, maybe they will be so moved by my words, that they will reduce my suspension by three weeks, and one day. I doubt it, but there was nothing wrong with a little wishful thinking on my part.

I showed the letter to my mother, which she promised to hand deliver tomorrow before work. She thought that the letter was kind of vague, and that I should have explained why I behaved in that manner to begin with, but whatever —it would have to suffice. I went to bed with a lot on my mind. I couldn't sleep, so I did what any normal fifteen-year-old boy would do under the circumstance: I pulled out my diary and started writing. Okay, so maybe I wasn't your typical 15-year-old, but I had to do something to unleash my racing thoughts.

Diary entry: #2 September 9th, 1988

Dear diary, or whatever you want to be called. It's been a while since my last entry, and a lot has happened. I met a dead girl, I met a dead girl's sister, I met a dead girl's sister's boyfriend, and I lost a friend, not to mention, that I told my teacher off, which got me suspended from school for a month. So, for the next month or so, it is going to be just you and I. Oh, and the dead girl: I can't help her, I can't even help myself. Goodnight, Diary...

I slept well, maybe, because I knew that I didn't have anywhere to be in the morning, or maybe, it was because I finally allowed myself to break free of Natalie. Whatever it was, I woke up rested and in a good mood. Mom had already left by the time I went downstairs, and most likely on her way to drop off my apology to the school. I made myself some coffee, and did some things that I haven't done in a while. My day was filled with reading (anything other than textbooks) drawing, some chores, and drinking more coffee than I probably should have.

When Mom arrived home from work later in the evening, I was sleeping on the couch, next to a sketch of a pterodactyl that I had been working on.

I peered out of my right eye, and saw her examining the picture, before putting it down.

"I see you started drawing again," she said, as she moved my feet, and sat down next to me.

"Yeah, I was bored."

82

"What else have you been doing?"

"Just relaxing mostly."

Her look turns more serious. "I have some good news, and I have some bad news, so, which one do you want to hear first?"

My eyes widened, and I ascended from my fetal position, ready to hear whatever news she had.

"Give me the good news first," I said anxiously.

"Okay, well… I stopped at your school to give your principal the apology letter. We had a nice conversation, and after some pleading on my part, he agreed to knock your suspension down to one week."

"Oh, that's great news," I said. "So, what's the bad news?"

"He agreed to knock time off your suspension, but-"

"Oh no," what is it?" I said, as I leaned in closer.

"It's not that bad really. He just wants you to talk to the school counselor three times a week."

"They want me to see a shrink?"

"Not a shrink—a counselor."

"Whatever, and you agreed to this?"

"I think this is the best option, considering the alternative."

"What alternative?" I asked.

"Mr. Healy, said if you don't agree to this then they would have no choice but to expel you from the school."

"Oh, that's wonderful," I said. "Do you really think that I am that messed up in the noggin, that I need to see a shrink three times a week?"

"I don't think you're messed up, but you have to admit— things haven't been going exactly smooth for you since we moved here."

"I admit, I do have my problems, and yes, I can get a little mouthy from time to time, but show me a teenager who doesn't do those things.

"C'mon, Ma, you can't expect me to behave like a saint. I'm sure that even St. Andrew had a few instances of unruly behavior as a teen. I think under the circumstances I have been pretty well behaved. I don't smoke, drink, throw parties, or have wild sex—not to mention, that I am home by curfew every night, and I've never been arrested."

"I know," she said, "you've been a really good kid, but I am seeing the early warning signs, Justin. I don't want you to end up like those troubled teens that I saw on the Geraldo show the other day. Please… just agree to do this for me."

I looked over at her, and I could see the sincerity in her eyes. I leaned in, and comforted her with a hug as she sobbed quietly.

"You win," I said. "I'll talk to the school counselor. Now please… don't cry anymore, because you're starting to look like that singer from *The Cure*."

She laughed, wiping the eyeliner away from her eyes.

The next morning, I told Mom about Seth, and how he heard Pete Tanelli in the boy's restroom, saying that something bad was going to happen to me over the weekend. She pried me for more details, but I had none to give. Mom brushed it off as kids talking trash, and told me to ignore the whole thing. I knew better than to just sweep it under the rug. Pete Tanelli was a firecracker waiting to pop, and his little band of popularities would pretty much do anything he said. Mom was working a double tonight at the restaurant, and I was to call her at work if there was an emergency.

Later in the evening, as I sat alone reading through one of Mom's old *Cosmopolitan* magazines, there was a knock on the front door that echoed throughout the noiseless house. I stood up immediately. I stared at the door for a moment, startled, before hiding behind the couch. I moved Ninja like, from the couch to the loveseat, to the end table, until I reached the window overlooking the porch. The curtain was slightly askew, allowing me to see movement of a shadow. The knocking continued and became heavier this time. I pressed my hand against my chest in a futile effort to calm myself.

"Justin?" a girl's voice called out. I knew the voice, it was Anna.

I was about to open the door, but then I remembered that she was going out with Pete, and if Pete was my enemy—then she was my enemy as well.

"Justin, open up. I know you're in there, I can hear you moving around," she said as she continued to pound on the door.

I got up from my hiding spot, and walked to the door. "What do you want, Anna? I have no new information for you."

"I want to talk to you for a minute, it's about Pete."

I opened the door to some extent, and peeked out to see her standing alone, postured perfectly like a figurine.

"Do you mind if I come in?"

I waved her in, and she immediately started apologizing for everything that Pete and her friends had put me through. She pulled twenty dollars from her pocket and placed it in my hand.

"What's this for?"

"It's for new tubes for your bike," she said.

"Thanks," I said, somewhat suspicious.

"You're welcome, but that's not the only reason why I stopped by your house."

"Is that, right?" I said. "So… what is it then?"

"I wanted to let you know, Pete, had something planned for you today, but I found out about it, and I put an end to it."

"What was he planning?" I asked.

"It doesn't matter now," she said, "I just wanted to apologize, and to let you know that you won't be harassed by us anymore."

"Why are you being so nice to me? Didn't you accuse me of knowing where Natalie was?"

"I don't know what happened to Natalie," she said, "but I can't just go around condemning everybody that came in contact with her. If you did have anything to do with it, I'm sure the cops will figure it out soon enough."

"What is that supposed to mean?"

"Nothing, it just means, that I'm sure the cops will figure the whole thing out eventually."

"Goodbye, Justin, and don't worry about Pete, I have him on a tight leash."

Anna smiled, as she walked out.

***

The next week was the longest week of my life. I stayed in the house the entire time to avoid Natalie, and to prevent myself from falling deeper into her mystery. I would have loved to help her, but I needed to get my own life together. Besides, if Amelia was right, then whoever murdered Natalie, would stop at nothing to keep the truth hidden. I wanted to help, but I also wanted to live to see my 16th birthday, which was only about a month away.

I mostly stayed in my room and kept myself busy by listening to music, or playing Nintendo on my small black and white television. Mom and I had been getting along much better since I agreed to see the school counselor. I thought the whole reason why she gave me that corny diary in the first place, was so that I could avoid seeing someone about my problems. Nevertheless, today was the day I returned to Grentan High, and I promised myself, that I would not let other people dictate my behavior from this point on.

Mom dropped me off at school, because the forecast was calling for a slight thunderstorm later in the day. I arrived at the school parking lot, and made my way past the usual cloud of cigarette smoke and muffled obscenities.

"Hey, Justin." I looked behind me to find Seth, standing there with this rueful grin on his face. I tried to speak but he interrupted me.

"Don't say anything, just listen."

I nodded me head, and he started talking.

"I'm sorry for being a coward, and for getting you suspended-"

Now I interrupted. "You didn't get me suspended."

"Yeah, I did," he said, "if I hadn't been such a lousy friend, then you wouldn't have stormed out of class the way you did."

"It's not your fault," I said, "I didn't have to act the way I did either".

"Well," Seth said, "I guess we both acted kind of foolish."

"Yeah, I guess we did. So, are we still friends? Because, quite frankly, I can't afford to lose another person in my life."

Seth smiled. "Me neither. Hey, if it makes you feel any better," Seth said, "everyone is talking about how you put Mr. Koval in his place."

"Really?" I said, somewhat amused, "what have they been saying?"

"I heard some of the students talking about how it took a lot of Moxie to say that to him, and how you were totally badass in the way that you just walked out like that."

"Well, I don't feel so badass. I'm more worried about seeing Mr. Koval again. I have a feeling that he is not going to make my life any easier this time around."

Seth and I started to walk to class, but not before Principal Healy spotted me and called me into his office.

"Please sit, Mr. Spencer."

I sat down on the wooden chair facing his executive, cushioned, leather office seat.

"Welcome back. I am sure you will be on your best behavior this time around?"

"Yes, sir."

"That's good, because we are a quiet, conservative school, and the last thing we need around here, is some *Johnny Rebel* stirring up the pot."

He grabbed a blue folder from his desk, and pulled out some papers. "Now... I made arrangements with Mr. Saunders, our school counselor, for you to meet with him at three today." "You will be meeting with him, three times a week, and he will be reporting your progress back to me. "I expect you to be honest with him, and respectful, regarding your treatment."

"Of course, sir."

"So, unless you have any questions for me, then you are free to go."

"No, sir."

"And Mr. Spencer," Mr. Healy added, "you're getting a second chance, please don't make me regret this."

"I won't, and thank you, sir."

I paced outside of homeroom for a few minutes, before finally entering. The room got unusually quiet, as I made my way to where Seth was seated. I was expecting a big speech from Mr. Koval, regarding my behavior, but it never came. After a few awkward minutes, things started to go back to the way they were. I guess everyone was waiting for an argument to develop, but when nothing happened, they got bored and went back to screwing off, or falling asleep. I tried to be respectful to Mr. Koval, by being attentive during his class, but he sure didn't make it easy on me. He spoke in that dry, monotone voice, that could tranquilize a fifteen-thousand-pound elephant, much faster than any drug could. I somehow managed to stay awake for the entire class, thanks to Seth, who thought it was funny to pelt Skittles at me every time my eyes grew heavy.

After class, I attempted to walk out with Seth, but Mr. Koval stopped me.

"Excuse me, Seth," Mr. Koval said. "But do you mind if I have a moment with Mr. Spencer?"

Seth looked at me, shrugged his shoulders, and walked out of the room.

"Mr. Spencer… I'll take it that Principal Healy spoke with you today before class?"

"Yes, he did, Mr. Koval."

"Well," Mr. Koval said, "I just wanted to say, that I received your letter asking for my forgiveness, and in return, I say to you, I do not accept your apology. Let me clear up a few things for you, Mr. Spencer, in case you were wondering how I managed to sustain my cool over the years.   "I have dealt with bigger, and tougher brats than you in my twenty some odd years here at Grentan High. I have been challenged, and cursed at, more times than I care to remember. So, if you think for a second that I will ever let you, or your hooligan friends get under my skin, then you have me pinned all wrong, Mr. Spencer."

"But, sir, I- "

"Don't interrupt me, Mr. Spencer. Now I am giving you another chance, because Mr. Healy has asked me to, but if it were up to me, I would have you scrubbing toilets with a toothbrush until your senior year.

"I have seen kids with your attitude, come and go from here, and the mouthy ones never get far in life. Most of them end up in jail, or working some dead-end job, with more children than they can afford to feed. So… with that said, Mr. Spencer, I would like to welcome you back. Here is a pamphlet regarding the rules here at Grentan. I am sure you will familiarize yourself with it during your spare time. Good day to you, sir—now get the hell out of my classroom."

My face was blood red, and my teeth were clenched so tight, that I thought for sure they'd shatter inside my mouth. How I managed to walk out of there, and hold my tongue for as long as I did, was anyone's guess.

Seth was leaning against the lockers as I stormed out of class.

"What happened in there?" Seth asked, "I could hear him yelling from out here."

"Nothing, the guy is a jerk, but, whatever. I don't need any more trouble from him, or anyone else for that matter. I just want to get through this school year, without any more incidents."

Seth snatched the pamphlet of rules out of my hand. "What is this?" Mr. Koval wants me to go over the rules during my spare time—can you believe that?"

Seth laughed, and tossed it in the trash. "Yeah, like that is ever going to happen." Seth suddenly put his arm in front of my chest to prevent me from walking any further. "Oh crap, don't look now, but our football hero is coming our way."

Pete Tanelli and a few of his teammates were headed straight towards us. Seth jerked at my shirt and attempted to drag me in the opposite direction.

"No," I said, "we are not running, I am through running."

Pete glanced down at me briefly, as he brushed alongside me, without saying a word.

"So, are you guys good now?" Seth asked.

"Good? Not exactly, but Anna promised me that he would stay out of my hair."

"Hey, that's great news, man—maybe things will get back to normal around here."

"I don't know," I said, "but I'm not taking anything for granted."

"Well, I better get to my next class," Seth said, "but I'll talk to you later."

By the time three o'clock rolled around, I was exhausted and just wanted to go home. I sluggishly lugged my book bag to the second floor to meet with the school counselor, Mr. Saunders. The door to his office was open, and I could see various books about psychology and the human condition stacked upon the floor. A painting of Sigmund Freud, hung lopsided from the lime green painted wall above his desk.

"May I help you?" he said. His voice was deep, and startled me, as I nervously looked over my shoulder.

"I am supposed to meet a Mr. Saunders," I said.

"You have come to the right place; I am Mr. Saunders. Won't you come in?"

11. A PASSING STORM

Mr. Saunders was a large man, of both width and height, and to a boy of my stature, his presence was a bit intimidating. He squeezed his buttocks into his office chair, which evidently was not suited for a man of his sizeable frame, and let out a sigh of relief when he was finally able to find a comfortable position.

"I presume you are my 3 p.m. appointment, Justin Spencer?"

"Yes," I said, "Mr. Healy stated that I would be attending three times a week."

He pulled out some folders from his desk, and examined each one before finding one with my name on it. "Oh Yes, here we are." He took his time looking over my file as if he were studying for the SATs. "So… if understand this correctly, you are not here on your own free will?"

"Yes," I said, "that's correct, sir."

As he read through my file, my focus was fixated on the unusual number of self-help books that lay stacked against the wall. Books on: *HOW to Be a Better Husband,* and *How to Be a Likable Person,* and a bunch of other drivel.

When he finished with my file, he placed it on top of his desk, and stood there silent for a moment. His fingers stroked his beard, and he stared at me, as if he wanted to speak, but was choosing his words carefully.

"It says here in your file, that you were disruptive during class, is this true?"

"I guess you can say that."

"You seem like a polite young man; why would you do something like that?"

"I had a lot going on, and I guess… I just kind of snapped."

"Well, Justin, everyone is entitled to one bad day—it's when those behaviors become routine that we need to worry. But let's see if we can figure out where the root of this problem lies, so we can go and dig it out, shall we?"

I told him everything, well, except that I had been talking to a dead girl, who needed my help in solving her murder. He listened intently, and took notes, as I spoke about growing up without my father, and how I hadn't made many friends, during my fifteen and half years on this planet. He mostly just listened, but chimed in a few times, briefly, to give me a few words of encouragement. The hour seemed to fly by, and neither one of us took notice how we were five minutes over our scheduled appointment. He seemed genuine, and I felt Like I was conversing with a friend, rather than a counselor.

By the time I got out of my counseling session with Mr. Saunders, the school parking lot was nothing more than a few scattered vehicles. I saw Mom waiting tolerantly for me in front of a row of orange cones. The first thing she asked me when I got in the car was, "How did the session go?"

`	I told her all about my day, and how Seth and I were talking again, and how I really felt comfortable talking with Mr. Saunders, and how Mr. Koval was still an ass, but I was willing to look past that, and just focus on school. I must have been feeling optimistic about things, because I couldn't shut up. Mom just smiled and nodded for the most part, while I talked nonstop the entire way home.

Diary entry: #3 Saturday-October 1ˢᵗ, 1988

Hello October, you are by far my favorite month of the year, and I'm not just saying that, because my birthday is on the 13ᵗʰ. I mean, it helps, but there is so much more to you than just that. The abundance of your vivid colors is by far, more spectacular here in Maine, more so, than I ever could have imagined. Your crisp, clean breezes that carry the scent of hot apple cider, and campfires, are evident with each passing day, and the dusky foliage surrounding Sherbrook has brought tourists to the area to witness the beauty of it all. The month of September had brought me a lot of up and down moments, but I have a feeling, that is all behind me now.

The past few weeks have been some of the best that I have experienced since moving to Maine. My counseling sessions with Mr. Saunders were helpful, and I felt that the advice he gave was more of a friend, than some condescending psychobabble bullshit. Seth and I have never been closer, and I believe that our little argument has only strengthened our friendship. He is the best friend that I ever had, or could hope for. Mom even had Seth over for dinner a few times, and vice versa, although, his mother is a terrible cook.

My grades were for the most part, acceptable, and I even succeeded on getting along with Mr. Koval, on most days. Anna kept her promise about keeping her boyfriend on a leash, and Natalie was nothing more than an afterthought. I avoided going to the playground, and the woods surrounding it; and when I remembered to do so—I slept with toilet paper in my ears, just in case she did get the urge to wake me up with pebbles again. Everything is great, and I can only picture things getting better from this day forward.

Mom and I spent the first day of October in downtown Sherbrook, where we took in the foliage and listened to some cover band play songs that Mom seemed to enjoy more so than myself. The aroma of funnel cake and apple cider overtook me, as I moved from one cobblestone street to the next.

"That smells so good," I said, as I pointed to a food vendor, who offered funnel cakes with a variety of toppings.

"The peach looks good," Mom said, as she moved in closer for a better look.

"Nah," I said, my mouth watering, "I want to try the strawberry with chocolate drizzle."

Mom grimaced and shook her head. "No thanks. Do we dare spoil our lunch with funnel cake?" Mom asked, while already grabbing money out of her purse.

"Spoil your lunch maybe, but I can eat all day—if you're buying?"

"Yes, may I help you?" the freckled young girl behind the counter said.

Mom started to order, when I felt a tap on my shoulder, and turned to see Natalie's father standing there with a wild look on his face. His eyes were dark as mud, and his breathing heavy, as he stared at me intensely. I was under the impression that he wasn't there to discuss the weather.

"Where is my daughter, you bastard?"

I tried to step away from him, but he took hold of my shirt with his left hand, and thrust his right-hand fingers into my throat. I gasped for air, as I struggled to break free from his tiger grip.

"What the hell are you doing?" Mom screeched, as she dropped the funnel cakes to the ground, and dashed to my rescue. Mom hopped onto Mr. Boyer's back, biting his ear so hard that he winced in pain, and released me from his hold.

"You bitch," he said, as he backhanded her, and she fell to the ground.

I laid sideways on the sidewalk, gasping for air, when I saw Mr. Boyer walking towards me.

"Help!" I shrieked.

A few fishermen working the docks nearby heard my pleas and came to our rescue. They managed to restrain Mr. Boyer until the cops came.

Officers from the Sherbrook Police Department showed up on scene, and took statements from a few witnesses who managed to see the whole incident unfold. Mom, for the most part, was just shaken by the ordeal, but otherwise, fine. Mr. Boyer continued to proclaim to the passerby's that I was guilty of hiding his daughter's whereabouts. A tall older cop with grey hair approached us with some paperwork to sign.

"Miss Spencer, I am Officer Plasky. I need to ask you if you wish to file charges against Mr. Boyer."

Without hesitation, Mom, declared, "Yes."

We both signed some forms regarding the truth in our statements, and we watched, as they asked Mr. Boyer to place his hands behind his back, before placing him under arrest.

I wanted to be angry with him for accusing me of knowing where his daughter was, but then I realized, that I did know where his daughter was. I knew that he would never see her alive again. My anger turned to guilt, and then sadness for him, because his daughter was dead, and possibly murdered by some psycho, who remained on the loose.

Mom remained a jittery mess for the rest of the night. I tried to sleep, but I could do nothing but lay in bed, and think about Natalie, and her father. Enough was enough already, I groaned. I can't do this anymore. I need to help Natalie find the truth about what happened to her on the night she died. Amelia was right—I was given this gift for a reason. I shouldn't be able to see and communicate with a dead girl, but I do, and there must be a reason for it all. I jumped out of bed and grabbed a jacket from my closet, and headed for the playground.

The night air was brisk, made cooler by the drizzling rain that had started a few minutes earlier. My breath was visible, and the light fog surrounding the woods made it difficult to see anything past 10 feet. My feet sunk into puddles of mud and soggy leaves, with each step towards the playground.

I was wet, and chilled, but determined, and I knew that I was here for a purpose. I was here to help, Natalie find peace.

"Natalie!" I shouted out into the darkness, my words sounding hollow through the fog and trees.

"I am sorry... I should've helped you. I understand if you are mad at me, but I'm not leaving this time—not until I help you move on."

The playground was a soggy mess of soil and leaves, that embedded itself into the treads of my shoes, and drenched my socks, making each step feel like I was drowning in quicksand.

"Where are you, Natalie? I'm here. I'm sorry, I will not abandon you again. Please--please, forgive me."

I felt a hand on my shoulder, but before I could turn around, my legs became jelly, and I dropped to my knees. Sadness and despair overwhelmed me, as tears trickled down my cheeks. The scenery turned dark, and the moon turned a blood red, as my eyes were suddenly not my own. I was seeing through the eyes of a dead girl; I was seeing through the eyes of Natalie.

I heard Natalie, speak to me. "Justin, don't be afraid. This is what I feel every day that I am trapped in this limbo. Do you feel it? The sorrow; the despair; the emptiness?"

"Yes," I said, while still crying uncontrollably.

"I am not here to bring you torment, but you must know how I feel, because you are the only one who can help me right now."

I continued sobbing. "I know, I'm so sorry, I'm ready to help." She

92

removed her hand, and all the suffering dissipated immediately. The darkness, that bounded my eyes, was lifted like a veil, as I staggered to my feet. I looked over at her, still unbalanced, but something was different. Her face was snowy, and translucent, and her body seemed to be scattering, like smoke from a cigarette, carried away by an evening breeze.

"What's going on?" I said. "What is happening to you?"

"My soul has started to evanesce from this world, and it's preparing itself for the netherworld."

"What?" I said. "What is that?"

"When someone's life is cut tragically short by the evil doings of another—the amount of time for someone to free the soul of suffering is limited. Each day that passes without resolve, the soul will continue to wander in torment, until more energy is lost, and eventually, the soul will fade into the Nether."

"What?" I asked. "I was told by a priest once, that people go to heaven, or hell—maybe purgatory, but this—this questions everything I was ever taught to believe in."

"There is a place beyond the light: a shimmering portal that echoes my mother's voice from within, but I cannot reach it on my own.
"It's beautiful, Justin, and the colors are unlike anything you have ever seen here on earth. The human mind cannot comprehend what I'm seeing, but it's so far out of reach. My mother is calling me home, and I can't get to her. It's like she's on an island, surrounded by miles of ocean, and I am stuck on the shore."

"Okay, that enough," I said, "I'm going to help you get out of here. I don't know how, but I have to believe there is reason behind this gift from God, or whoever, and I believe that reason is to get you back with your mother."

"Time is running out; I don't think I can hold on much longer."

"You need to try to hold on for me, Natalie. What do you remember about the night you were murdered?"

"I don't know."

"Please, Natalie—think. You say you were murdered, but how can you be certain; are you sure it wasn't something else that ended your life?"

"I can feel it," she said, "it's a sense of complete desolation and grief. I showed you what it felt like. I don't know how to explain it, but, I know my life ended in a violent way."

"Please try to concentrate," I said, "I need your help if you ever want to be reunited with your mother."

She paused for a moment, completely lost in thought, and then her eyes widened, and she blurted out the name: "Anna."

"Anna?" I asked. "What about her?"

"I remember that I was with Anna."

"Ok, this is good," I said, "what else do you remember?"

"It was our 16TH birthday," Natalie said, as she paced back and forth - her body becoming eerily lost within the mist. "We were talking about our birthday plans and my father-"

"What about your father?"

"Anna mentioned that Dad was going to meet us at Riccardo's restaurant for our annual birthday dinner."

"What happened at Riccardo's, Natalie?"

There was a great deal of concentration written on her face, as she placed her index fingers from each hand, between her temples, and closed her eyes. She then opened her eyes and her pupils grew large. And as if she had come to some revelation, her jaw dropped and she whispered, "It was Anna--It was Anna," she said again, as though she was trying to convince herself. "Anna murdered me."

12. FAMILY TIES

The rain started to pick up, and the wind sent it whipping against my body like an angry Poseidon. My teeth chattered, and I started to shiver, but I was too focused on Natalie to start worrying about myself.

"No," I said, "you must be mistaken, why would Anna murder you?"

"I don't know, but she murdered me. She wanted me dead."

"Are you sure Anna was the one who murdered you? Because we need to be certain if I'm going to be making accusations as serious as that to the cops."

"Yes, it was her."

"What do you remember?"

"It was our birthday, and I was getting ready to have dinner at Riccardo's restaurant with my family. Anna picked me up at home, and informed me that Dad was running late from work but that he would meet us at the restaurant."

"It still doesn't mean that she murdered you," I said.

"Wait… I'm not finished. She was driving recklessly through the back roads, and she had this nervous smile on her face, and I remember asking her why she was driving us away from the restaurant. She just smiled at me and said that it was a birthday surprise, and that I should prepare myself for the biggest shock of my life. I was so excited, and could barely sit still in my seat, as we drove miles away from the city. "We finally stopped at a long, empty, stretch of road. There were no houses or street lamps that I could see - only fields of darkness, surrounded by trees. She killed the headlights on the car and told me to get out. I was confused, and asked her why, but she told me to trust her, so, I did. We walked up a long, dirt driveway that led to an abandoned barn. I walked alongside her, as she pointed the way with her flashlight. I got to the entrance, and stopped to look back at Anna.

"She told me to walk in first, because there was something waiting for me behind the doors. I pulled the latch back, expecting to find a car for my 16th birthday, and then… everything went black."

"So, what do you remember after that?" I asked.

"I remember waking up, and not being able to see. As I struggled to make sense of what was happening, I realized that I had been blindfolded in the trunk of a car. I could feel the bumps on the road, and hear The Smiths playing over the car radio.

"My hands were tied behind my back, and my mouth covered with tape.

My head throbbed with pain and my legs were bound together by rope. I rocked back and forth, as I tried to break free from my restraints. I finally managed to loosen the knot around my wrist, and rip the blindfold from my eyes. I pulled the tape from my mouth, and took a deep breath, as I loosened the rope around my legs.

"For a moment, I thought that this was some sort of sick birthday joke that my sister had planned, but then I felt my head, and the wet blood still gushing from my wound, and I knew then that this was no joke. I felt around the darkness for anything that might be useful to defend myself, and managed to find a tire iron. I clutched my weapon to my chest, and waited for someone to open the trunk. I didn't want to die that night, and I was prepared for the fight of my life. The car stopped and I heard a man's voice.

"I couldn't make out what was being said, but then I heard two doors close, and the car started to move again. There was an argument coming from inside the car, but it was unclear to me due to the radio drowning out most of what was being said. The car stopped again, and the engine grew quiet. My heart was pounding so loud, that I was almost certain they could hear it. Tears of betrayal turned to rage and anger, as I sat there waiting for anyone to open the trunk. I could hear whispers of people outside, and then I heard the key going into the lock.

"I held on to my weapon, and tightened my grip, while waiting to unleash all my fury on the first person I saw."

"The trunk opened, and my sister and Pete stood above me. I leapt out of the trunk like a wild animal being chased by a pack of wolves. I felt someone grab my shoe, and without thinking, I swung the tire iron down onto their hands. It was Pete, and he let out a piercing cry that carried throughout the woods. I managed to get back to my feet, and started running, as fast as my legs would carry me. All I could see were trees, and the deeper I got, the thicker it became.

"Branches swung by like bats, and struck me with such force that my face started to become bruised with cuts, that dripped warm blood into my eyes. I could hear footsteps behind me, and twigs breaking beneath me, as I continued to run through the blackness of the night. I started to feel weak and out of breath, as my running had become nothing more than a brisk walk. I could hear the footsteps approaching, as they came closer and closer, and then: nothing. I found refuge behind a massive pine, and prayed silently to myself for them to give up.

"There was movement a few feet away from me, and as it got louder and louder. I knew that I had to move. I managed to get to a nearby tree, and ducked quietly from one tree to another. I got down on my stomach, and slithered like a snake through the dirt. It was then that I realized where I was."

"Where were you?" I asked.

"I was at my childhood place… my playground."

Natalie stood there staring silently at the ground for a moment, as the rain continued to fall around her, and through her.

"Natalie?" I said, "what happened at the playground?"

She picked her head up, and started where she had left off.

"The swing rocked back and forth like a pendulum," she said, "as I stood there, hypnotized by its movement. I could hear footsteps approaching, but could find no strength in my beaten body to move.

"I can't do this, Justin- I just can't."

"Natalie," I said, "please don't lose me- what happened?"

She continued, "I started to walk towards the swing, and that's when I saw it."

"What did you see?" I asked.

"A hole--a hole big enough to hide a body. I stood there looking down into it, and I knew that this was meant for me. I then saw Pete coming out from the woods. He cornered me, and called out for my sister. They both had a look in their eyes that said everything to me, without saying anything. I saw evil that night, Justin, I don't think I ever saw anything so wicked before, and there was nothing I could do to stop it from devouring me. They stood there silently watching for a moment with these halfcocked smiles on their faces, and then…"

"What Natalie?" I said, "you need to finish the story."

"Pete pulled out a handgun and pointed it at me," she said. "They both looked at one another and smiled, like two hunters, celebrating the capture of their prey."

"I stood there in a frozen state - too afraid to move - and not enough strength to run. I wiped the blood that had been dripping into my eyes away from my face. Pete moved in closer, and then Anna took the gun from him. For a moment, I thought that she had a change of heart, and that I was going to somehow make it out of this alive. She looked at him with this sinister smile, then pointed the gun at my head, before cocking it back and firing the shot.   "I don't remember anything after that."

"I can't believe what I'm hearing," I said. "So that's why your sister was trying to put the focus of the investigation on me. She figured I would go to jail, and her and Pete would just move on with their perfect little lives. Do you know why your sister wanted you dead? Was there money involved?"

"I don't know why," she said, "it couldn't have been money, because I had none."

"I'm sorry, Natalie; I don't even know what to say to comfort you right now, because, there are no words."

"You don't need to say anything," she said, "just please, promise me, that you won't leave me this time."

"I promise. Pinky swear," I said, as I held out my right-hand pinky finger.

She gave me one of those half smiles that you give to someone when you're feeling crappy, but are trying hard not to smile because it wouldn't go well with your depressed state.

"I would've really liked to have known you before all this happened," I said. "I think we could've been pretty good friends."
Her face lightened up a bit, and she said, "I do too."

I started kicking away debris from the ground, and carefully looked over the area. "If your sister murdered you at this spot, then your body is buried somewhere around here. That is why you can't move on from this place. Do you remember where the hole was?"

Natalie pointed to where the swing hung, and the hair on the back of my neck stood up, as a sick feeling in my stomach overcame me. I carefully looked down for any signs of a burial, but the stinging rain, and mud soaked branches and leaves, made it impossible to do so. "Okay Natalie, I am going to get help, and then we are going to put this thing to rest once and for all."

"Wait," she said, "you can't do that."

"Why?" I said. "I thought you wanted my help - this is the only way."

"I do want your help," she said, "but you can't just run into the police station and say, 'I know where Natalie Boyer's body is buried.' Do you think for a second that they will believe you, when you tell them you were sent there by the ghost of the victim?"

My enthusiasm suddenly dwindled, as I realized that she was right. Nobody would believe such a concocted story about my abilities to communicate with a dead girl, who needed my help to solve her murder, so she can rest in peace.

I looked over at Natalie, with the rain falling through her, her hair and clothes perfectly dry, and her body fading ever so slightly.
"No, I have to try. Don't you see, Natalie? If I do nothing, then you get stuck in the Netherworld, and I'm not about to let that happen. How much longer do you think we have before your body disappears forever?"

"I don't know," she said. "It seems like I fade a bit more with each passing day."
"Okay, I'm going to figure something out," I said. "I will be back here before 24 hours, and If you don't hear from me, then expect the worst."
"What are you planning on doing?" she said.

"I don't know, but it better be damn good."

I ran like my life depended on it, and made it home right before three in the morning. Mom was still sleeping as I snuck inside. I have to think. What am I going to do to help Natalie in the middle of the night? I wondered. I paced nervously from room to room, thinking about the most reasonable way to explain to someone about Natalie's murder, without coming off as completely insane, not to mention, guilty. I picked up the phone and sat there for several seconds, listening to it beep into my ear. I dial the nine, and hesitate for a moment, before pressing one twice.

"911, what is your emergency?" the female dispatcher asked.

"I'm not really sure."

"You're not really sure if this is an emergency?"

"No," I said, "I'm just not really sure how to say this-"

"Sir, is this an emergency or not?"

"Yes," I hesitated, "someone has been murdered."

"Who is the victim, sir?"

"Natalie Boyer, her name is Natalie Boyer."

"Where did the murder take place, sir?"

"It's somewhere behind my house; in the woods behind my house."

"I am going to need your name and address, sir?"

I stood there silent; too afraid to speak and get involved in something form which there would be no coming back.

"Sir?" the dispatcher said. "Hello? Are you still there, sir?"

I hung up the phone, and stood there just staring at it, as if I made the biggest mistake of my life. After about two minutes, the phone started to ring. At once, I picked it up, and immediately slammed it back down. I snatched the cord from the wall and tossed the phone into the kitchen drawer. I scurried to the front window expecting to see a hundred cops show up at any minute with their guns drawn. I heard footsteps coming from above, and then making their way down the steps, and into the living room.

"What is going on here?" Mom said, half asleep, with curlers in her hair and the left half of her face imprinted with the design of her pillowcase.

"Mom, I need to talk to you-"

She interrupted, "Did I hear the phone ring, or was I dreaming?"

"Mom, you need to listen to me-"

"Can it wait until tomorrow sweetie; I am too exhausted for a long conversation right now."

"Listen to me for once," I said, "that was the cops on the phone."

Her eyes widened and her lips pursed at the very mention of cops.

"What did you do, Justin-Phillip-Spencer?"

"Nothing bad, I swear."

She folded her arms in front of her chest, "Don't you lie to me young man."

Before I could answer, we both looked over at the window to see flashing lights pulling up our driveway. My worst fears were becoming a reality. I ran to the window and moved the curtains to the side, as Mom peered over my shoulders to witness a half dozen squad cars pulling up the driveway. She gave me a look that I knew all too well, and it meant I was in big trouble. The officers rushed out of their cruisers and to our front door with their weapons drawn. Mom immediately let them in, as they flashed their badges at us - and before I knew it - the house was filled with cops and detectives. An older gentleman with a long brown trench coat and wearing a faded brown fedora introduced himself as Detective Mickey Collins.

"What is the meaning of all this?" Mom said, panicky.

"Miss Spencer," Detective Collins said, "we received a call from this residence about a possible murder."

Mom looked over at me and just shook her head in disappointment.

"What murder?" Mom asked.

"That's what we need to find out ma'am. Apparently, the male voice on the phone said they had information about the murder of Natalie Boyer." "The girl went missing a few months ago, and she hasn't been seen or heard from since- except of course for your boy, Mrs. Spencer."

Detective Collins looked me up and down, and then paused for a moment to look over my shoulder at some pictures of Mom and I on the wall. "Do you have information regarding Natalie Boyer, young man?"

I looked over at Mom for some help, but she looked away, and sat down. "I don't know," I said.

"Son, a father is worried sick about his missing daughter, so if you have anything you need to say, then for God sake; say it." Detective Collins continued, "As of right now, this is a case of a missing person, but if someone did something to that girl, then we need to know."

Mom was still not looking at me, but I could tell her ears where tuned into our conversation. There was no turning back from this, I thought, the damage was done, so I figured I'd better start talking.

"Okay," I took a deep breath and let out a sigh, "I know where Natalie is buried."

Mom's jaw dropped when she heard me speak the words, and her body went limp, as she collapsed to the floor.

I ran over to help but Detective Collins stopped me, with a quick arm to my chest.

"Someone help her off the floor!" Detective Collins shouted. One of the officers grabbed her from behind and pulled her up, while another grabbed her feet, as they carried her to the couch.

"How about we take a ride down to the station," Detective Collins said, "and you can tell me all about what happened to Natalie."

Mom sat up from the couch, and somehow managed to find the strength to walk over to me and grab my arm. "Don't go, Justin."

"Ma'am," one of the officers said, as he escorted her into the kitchen. "Don't say anything, Justin!" Mom hollered. "Don't you dare say anything. I'm going to call a lawyer."

"It's ok, Mom, don't worry."

I told her not to worry, but I was worried. How the heck was I going to convince this detective that I had nothing to do with this, without coming off as incredible? Detective Collins seemed to be a straight by the book kind of guy, and I couldn't imagine what he was going to think of my wild tales.

Detective Collins escorted me out of the house and allowed me to sit in the front of his squad car with him as we made our way to the station.

I was led to a back door at the end of the hall, that had *Interrogation Room* printed above it.

"Wait here," the detective said, "and I will be with you momentarily."

The room was nothing more than a blinding light, reflecting off colorless walls, and a table overlooking a large two-way mirror. The intensity of light in the room, made me squint as I sat down and stared at my reflection in the mirror. I sat there alone with my thoughts, as I tried to come up with the most logical way of retelling Natalie's story to Detective Collins. After several minutes, Detective Collins walked in, and sat across from me. He handed me a can of Ginger Ale and a bag of low sodium potato chips. "Sorry, it's all that was left in the vending machine," he said.

"It's ok," I said. "I don't have much of an appetite right now anyway." He pulled a cigar out of his pocket and asked if I minded. I shook my head, as he lit up and put a yellow folder with Natalie's picture down in front of me and pointed to it.

"Do you know this girl, Justin?"

I sat silent for a few seconds before answering, "I don't really know how to say this, without coming off as crazy."

"Why don't you try me," he said, "I've heard plenty of stories during my many years on the force, so nothing really surprises me anymore.

I swallowed. "Do you believe in ghosts, Detective?"

"Ghosts?" he asked. "I don't quite understand where you're going with this."

"Please, Detective… it's important."

He puffed on his cigar, filling the air with smoke, as he stood there watching me. It was as if he was looking straight through me, and I looked away, no longer able to maintain eye contact. "I guess I never really gave it much thought," he said. "I suppose it's possible, but, I'm more of a seeing is believing kind of guy. I've never been much into the whole faith of a higher being, or whatever. Why do ask?"

"Well," I said, "it kind of has everything to do about why I'm here."

"I'm not following," he said.

"Ok, Detective." I took a deep breath. "I'm going to say this, so please try to listen with an open mind."

"You have my full attention," he said.

The interrogation lasted well over two hours, and by the time I was done, the night had turned to day. Detective Collins rubbed his eyes and snuffed his cigar into the ashtray. "So, just that I'm hearing this right: Natalie Boyer's spirit came to you, and wanted you to help solve her murder. Then you say, she told you about how her sister and her boyfriend murdered her, and buried her remains at the playground behind your house?"

I nodded, and took notice of how ridiculous the whole story sounded being replayed back to me like a tape player. Detective Collins took a long, hard look into my eyes. "And you're the only person who can see her? Because some old woman told you, that you have a gift?"

"Yeah," I said, "something like that."

He rubbed his temples, and pulled out another cigar. "I have got to tell you, Justin; I heard some pretty wild shit in my time, but your story... well, that takes first place."

"I know it sounds crazy, Detective, but it's all true."   "Okay,"   he said, "let me send some men down to the spot where you claim she is buried, and see if we can figure this thing out. In the meantime, I am going to release you back into the custody of your mother, but only under one condition: You can't leave town. Do you understand that?"

"Yes sir" I said.

Mom was waiting out front, still wearing her pajamas, and drinking a coffee that one of the cops made for her. She ran over to me as I walked out, and gave me a hug while trying not to spill her coffee. "I was worried sick," she said, looking me over to make sure I was still intact. "What did you tell them?"

"I'm exhausted," I said, "can it wait until we get home?"

"Sure," she said.

When we arrived home, I relayed to Mom the same story that I told Detective Collins. When I finished, she started to cry. "Justin, do you realize what you have done? You have implicated yourself in a murder."

"No," I said, "I'm telling the truth."

"I can't believe you are doing this to me," she said. "Why are you doing this to me?"

Mom started to scurry around the house, pulling stuff out of drawers and cabinets, and tossing papers and magazines to the floor without regard.

"What are you doing?" I said.

"I'm looking for a phonebook."

"Why?"

"Because, we need to find you a lawyer."

"You're not listening to me," I said, "I told you that I didn't do anything."

"Is it drugs, Justin? Did someone at school get you to try drugs?"

"No," I scoffed, "it's not drugs." I grabbed her hand and attempted to stop her from looking for a moment. "Listen, Mom... it's not drugs, and I'm not crazy. "Everything that I told you, was the honest to God truth. Natalie was murdered and she needed my help."

"Oh my God," she said, "do you hear yourself? The only thing that might be able to save you is an insanity plea."

She pushed my hand away and continued her search for a phone book.

"I didn't do anything; do you hear me?"

"Justin, I need you to be honest with me. Did you murder that girl?"

"No, I didn't murder anyone!"

"Oh God," she said, "and to think that I had her poor father arrested."

"I can't listen to this anymore," I said. "I'm going to my room."

My bedroom seemed foreign to me, as I sat there looking up at the ceiling, and tracing the designs of the crown molding in my head. I was exhausted but my mind would not rest. I started to curse, under my breath, this so-called gift of mine. It was no gift, and if it was, then it must've been sent first class, by the devil himself. After about an hour of lying in bed with my eyes closed, I eventually fell asleep.

I awoke around 4 p.m., to my mother screaming at me to wake up. "The cops are here," she said, while shaking my body, "get up!"

"What are you talking about?" I said.

"They have a search warrant, and they are tearing the house apart. "Get up!"

"I'm up--I'm up," I said, as I jumped to me feet. I heard the march of footsteps making their way upstairs, and the static of chatter coming from walkie talkies in the distance. Several officers marched into my room with empty bags that had *evidence* written on them, and started tearing things apart. Another cop informed Mom and I to sit downstairs, where we weren't allowed to touch anything, or interfere in any way, or we would be arrested. Detective Collins was waiting for us downstairs and told us to take a seat.

"What is going on here?" Mom demanded.

"Listen, Ma'am, I am only doing my job. Your son gave us information about where a body was buried, and now we are doing a routine search."

"So, you found the body?" Mom said.

"Yes, Ma'am, we did exhume human remains. We are waiting to hear back from the coroner's office to identify, if in fact, the remains are those of Natalie Boyer."

"Oh my God," my mom said, as she put her hands over her eyes. "I can't believe this is happening." She then looked over at me with tears falling from her face and said, "What did you do, Justin? My God- what did you do?"

An officer approached Detective Collins, whispering in his ear, before handing him my diary.

"Hey, that's mine," I said in protest.

"I'm sorry, but this is evidence now," the detective said.

"What did you write in there?" Mom asked.

"It doesn't matter," I said, "those are my personal thoughts and feelings - what gives you the right to take my personal stuff?"

Detective Collins pulled out his badge and put it directly in front of my face. "This give me the right. I can tear the floorboards out and knock down every wall in this house if I wanted to - and in case I failed to mention: I also happen to have a search warrant signed by a judge, so don't give me any shit about doing my job."

"No," Mom pleaded, "please don't destroy the house. This isn't our home; we are just renting."

Detective Collins pulled out a cigar and lit up, without asking if it was okay to do so. "Listen, Ma'am. The last thing I want to do is tear apart your little home you made for yourself here, but there is a dead body buried behind your house, and a boy that is claiming to be in contact with a ghost. I need to obtain as much evidence as I can if I am going to solve this case, and either proclaim your son's innocence, or guilt.

"I am not trying to come off as a hard-ass, but a girl is missing, and my main concern right now, is to help a grieving father bring home his missing daughter."

"What about Anna and Pete?" I said, "are you just going to let them get away with this?"

"No, they are being interviewed right now as we speak, but it doesn't mean they are guilty of anything, unless we have evidence."

"I gave you all the evidence you need," I huffed.

"A statement from a ghost is not going to stand up in court, Justin. This is the real world, and we need real evidence. Everyone just sit tight, and let us finish our jobs," the detective said, "so you two can have your house back."

After several hours of searching, the cops finally left our home. Everything was in disarray, as we walked throughout the house. Papers and clothes were tossed with little respect; plates and glasses were out of their cupboards, and food was left scattered on the kitchen table. Every inch of every room was a mess, and it was a little too much for Mom to handle. She grabbed a plate discarded on the floor and smashed it against the wall. "Do you see what you have done here?" she said.

"Mom," I said, "I know you think that I messed up, but you have to believe me; my intentions were to help Natalie."

"Natalie?" she said. "I don't want to hear another word about Natalie. Take a good look around, Justin, because you caused all this. I saved, and sacrificed to get us away from William, so that you could have a better life and a chance at a childhood."

"Childhood?" I scoffed. "That's funny, Mom, because I never had the chance to be a child. I always had to be the adult, because someone had to be. So, don't talk to me about being a child, because in case you haven't noticed - it's a little too late for that now."

I started to put my jacket on, but before I could finish, she grabbed it off my shoulders. "You're not leaving this house," she said.

"Oh, yes I am," I said, as I snatched the jacket out of her hands and put it on.

"If you leave this house," she said, "then don't even think about coming back."

I tore the jacket off and threw it to the floor. The promise I made Natalie to return would have to wait; besides, the whole playground was probably an active crime scene by now.

"Fine," I said, "I'm going upstairs."

"No, you're not," she said, "you're going to help me clean up this mess that you have brought into our home."

"Fine," I said, "you want me to clean up the mess - I will clean up the mess - but I'm starting in my room."

I never saw Mom this angry before, and it wasn't a pleasant sight. She had every right to be pissed at me, but I was trying to do a selfless thing for once in my life. The only problem was: nobody believed me.

We worked into the night; fueled on coffee, and anger, and by 2 a.m. we had finally finished.

"You better get some sleep," Mom said, as she put away the last of the remaining silverware.

I went to bed without saying a word.

I slept a few hours, and by 7 a.m. I was ready for school. Mom was downstairs on the couch, her eyes bloodshot, and her hair disheveled. "What are you doing up?" she said.

"I'm going to have some coffee, and then ride my bike to school."

"No, you're not," she said, "you're staying home until the cops figure this whole thing out. I don't need that girl's family coming after you."

"I am going to school Mom."

"No, you're not," she said, "I don't want to leave work early to pick you up at school, because of some misunderstanding. Now stay here, and try to stay out of trouble. Can you manage that much for one day?"

"So, your plan is to keep me locked up in this house, until the cops come to lock me up for good?   "Thanks, Mom, I really appreciate it."

She shook her head and let out a long sigh. "I'm going to work, and when I get home, you better be here."

I waited for her car to pull out of the driveway, then I grabbed my backpack off the floor and headed to school.

Maybe it was my paranoia, but when I arrived at school, I could feel the sting of a hundred eyes gawking at me as I made my way to homeroom. I didn't see any sign of Pete or Anna, but I was sure they figured out by now who told the cops about them. I wanted to avoid them like my life depended on it, because, in all actuality, it did. Anyone who would do something so cold, and callous to a sister, and a sweet girl such as Natalie, had to be deeply disturbed.

Seth was in class with his head down as I walked to my seat. His eyes widened and his mouth dropped slightly at the sight of me. "What are you doing here?" he whispered.

"It's a school day, silly," I said, knowing damn well what he meant.

"No," Seth said, "I mean, what are you doing here? Anna and Pete are looking for you, and they are not happy at all."

13. UNLUCKY

"They are pissed, because you had Anna's father arrested, and for accusing them of killing Natalie. You shouldn't be here."

"It's all true Seth - they killed her - and I'm not going to let them get away with it."

"If I were you, man, I would take off right now, before it's too late."

"I'm not running anymore," I said, "they can look for me all they want. I'm not hiding, because I did nothing wrong."

"Okay, man, it's your funeral. All I am saying," Seth added, "is that Pete is the star quarterback, and Anna is head cheerleader, and you… well, no offense, but you are just some kid from Scranton."

Thanks a lot," I said, "but I'm not going to let a few thugs run me into hiding. I've been hiding my entire life. I'm through with hiding - so drop it."

Mr. Koval struck my desk with his ruler. "Is there a problem here, Mr. Spencer?"

"No problem, sir," I said, embarrassed.

"Are you sure? Because, I can hold off on our important announcements to accommodate you, and your conversation with Seth here."

"I said… there is no problem, Mr. Koval."

"Well," he said, "just in case, why don't you go see the school counselor and have a little talk with him."

"No thanks, I'm fine."

"That was not an option, Mr. Spencer," he said sternly.

Several students were snickering as I went into the hallway. I started to walk to the counselor's office, when suddenly my name was announced over the loudspeaker: *"Justin Spencer, please report to the Principal's office - Justin Spencer to the Principal's office."*

"Oh great," I said, as I turned back. The Principal's office was in the opposite direction, and I could only imagine why he wanted to see me this time. The halls were mostly empty, but then I saw Pete and a few of his jock friends walking towards me.

"Hey," Pete said, "look who it is. It's our hometown hero: Justin Spencer." His crew blocked my path as I tried to move past them, and I quickly found myself thrown against a wall full of lockers. My eyes wandered desperately for some help, but it was just them and I. "Thanks guys," Pete said, "I will take it from here."

His face was directly in front of mine, as he moved in closer and proceeded to sniff my neck. Disgusted, I try to push him away, but he was too strong. "Do you smell that, guys? That, my friends, is the smell of fear."

The jocks just laughed stupidly as they kept watch for oncoming teachers. "It seems the new kid here," Pete said, as he prodded my chest with his finger, "likes to poke his nose into other people's business. He is a regular Magnum, P.I. this one. Trying to solve crimes, and making accusations that have nothing to do with him."

He grabbed my bookbag from my shoulders and tossed it to the floor. "You see, Justin, you can try to be the Sherlock Holmes of Sherbrook, but a good detective knows when he has been beat." He moved in closer and whispered in my ear: "You lose, dweeb. I suggest you run along now little doggie," Pete said, as he loosened his grip.

I reached for my backpack lying on the floor, and started running down the hallway as Pete and his friends made loud dog noises. "Woof—woof—woof."

I arrived at Principal Healy's office scared, and out of breath.

"What's the matter with you, son? Don't you know there is no running in the halls?" Mr. Healy said.

"I just wanted to get here on time, sir," I lied.

"Sit down, Justin. A Detective Collins called me and asked me to have you wait for him here until he arrives."

"What does he want me for?" I asked.

"He said that he will be picking you up shortly to bring you in for questioning. Are you in some sort of trouble, Justin?"

"I don't know," I said, "I don't know anything anymore."

"I better call your mother about this."

"She knows already, Mr. Healy, and it's a long story - so please: just drop it. I don't expect you, or anyone else to understand, because I only make myself seem crazier with every syllable that comes out of my mouth."

Before he could respond, Detective Collins knocked on the door. "Hello, Mr. Healy, I believe we spoke on the phone briefly."

"Yes, nice to meet you Detective," Mr. Healy said, as they shook hands.

"Well," Detective Collins said, "we won't take up any more of your valuable time. So, are you ready, Justin?"

"Ready for what?" I said.

"I need to bring you in for some questioning - it shouldn't take too long."

"Listen," I said, "if you're going to arrest me, then just do it now and get it over with."

Detective Collins smiled nervously at Mr. Healy, and then turned his attention back to me. "Justin, nobody is going to jail today; I can promise you that. I just have a few more questions for you down at the precinct."

Mr. Healy interrupted. "Is there anything we at the school need to be worried about, Detective?"

"Not a thing, Mr. Healy, but I will give you a call later and we can have a little chat. Thanks again," Detective Collins said, as he tilted his hat to Mr. Healy and escorted me out of the building.

I arrived at the station with Detective Collins leading the way back to the interrogation room. "When do I get my diary back?" I asked.

"That is one of the reasons why I wanted you to come down today," the detective said, "so we can talk about your diary." He opened the door to the interrogation room, where a middle-aged bald man, wearing a cheaply made suit and frameless glasses, was seated with loads of paperwork in front of him. He rose when we entered, and introduced himself as Dr. Michael Brandon.

"I will leave you two alone for now," the detective said, as he slipped out the door.

"Please, Justin, won't you take a seat," Dr. Brandon said. His voice was high and whiny, and he looked as though he could've played an extra in *"The Revenge of the Nerds"* movie.

"So, you're a doctor?" I asked.

"Yes, but I am not a surgeon, or anything like that. My expertise is the human mind."

"So, you're a neurologist?"

He chuckled slightly. "No, I am a psychiatrist. I work mostly with adolescents, but I have a few adult patients as well."

"That's nice," I said, "but what am I doing here?"

"Well, Justin, I was asked to look over your diary by Detective Collins, and to speak with you personally. Do you mind speaking with me today?"

"Do I have a choice?"

"Yes, you have a choice, but if you want to help yourself, and that young girl, then I would advise you to please consider going through with this interview."

"Okay, but you're just going to think I'm nuts, like everyone else."

"Well, we don't like to use the word 'nuts', Justin. Everyone has problems, some more serious than others, but we never consider anybody nuts, or crazy. Some people are just born with deficiencies, not of their own doing, and are treated accordingly with proper medications."

"So, you want to drug me up?" I scoffed at the very idea.

"No," Dr. Brandon said, "not at all. I would just like to ask you a few questions about this diary.".

I crossed my arms and slouched down into the seat. I figured that if they were going to make me sit here, I might as well get comfortable.

"Okay, let's get this over with," I said.

"Now, Justin, you wrote in your diary about a dead girl. Who was the dead girl you were referring to?"

"Natalie Boyer," I said, as I stared at the light reflecting off his bald scalp.

"Okay," he said, scribbling notes in his chart. "And what made you believe she was dead, when her family and the police assumed she was missing?"

"It doesn't matter," I said, "because you're not going to believe me anyway."

"I am not here to cast judgement down on you, that is for the police to decide. I am merely here, because some of your words are concerning."

"Concerning?" I scoffed. "Concerning to who?"

"Whom," Dr. Brandon said.

"What?" I said, as I shrugged.

"It's concerning to whom," he said, "you said concerning to who."

I wanted to reach over and deck him something good in that smug, goofy looking face of his, but I bit my tongue instead. He took off his glasses and placed them on the table, next to his empty coffee mug. He then put his hand under his chin and gently rubbed it with his index finger and thumb, as if he was deep in thought.

It appeared to me, Dr. Michael Brandon believed he was in the same class with other brilliant minds of the 20th century, and all he needed was one head case like myself to push him into the national spotlight.
"Do you believe in ghosts, Justin?"

"Do you believe in ghosts, Michael?" I said sarcastically.

"I believe in Science, and please - call me Dr. Brandon. Now I asked you a question, so will you please answer it?"

"Yes, I'm aware," I said, "but I also asked you a question."

"This interview is not about whether or not I believe in the paranormal, but about what you believe in," he said.

"I believe in a lot of things, Dr. Strange. For instance: I believe psychiatrists are not real doctors, I believe that psychiatry is a useless profession, and I believe this interview is over."
I stood up and pushed in my seat, and just as I was about to make my exit, Detective Collins stopped me. "You're not leaving here until you talk to Dr. Brandon." He puffed on his cigar, inhaled and then exhaled into my face.

"Now sit down, and answer his questions," Detective Collins said sternly.

I didn't wait for him to ask twice. I sat down and we continued the interview.

Dr. Brandon was trying to find his composure, even though he looked as though he wanted to leap from his chair and strangle me with his tie. "Now, if you would please answer the question: Do you believe in ghosts?"

"Yes, I believe in ghosts - are you happy now?" I said facetiously. "Next question, Doc - I don't have all day."

Dr. Brandon looked over his shoulder, and into the two-way mirror, as if he was going to motion someone to come in, and restrain me at any moment.

"Okay, Justin, you mentioned the dead girl in your diary and how she communicates with you: do you believe that?"

"Of course I believe it," I huffed. "It's the only reason why I'm sitting in this blinding room and talking to some quack who doesn't have a clue about what's going on."

Dr. Brandon stood up, unable to control his emotions any further, and started to wave his right index figure in my face. "You listen here: I have given lectures at some of the finest universities in the country, and I am not going to be disrespected by some--some...murderer."

Now I was out of my seat and ready to defend myself. "How dare you call me a murderer!" I shouted, "You know nothing about me." Three cops, along with Detective Collins, rushed into the room and grabbed me by my arms. I was still screaming and kicking as the cops dragged me out the door.

"Put him in the holding cell for now!" Detective Collins shouted to the two officers holding my wrists. "I'll figure out what to do with him in a bit."

The two cops pushed me into a 6 by 8-foot cell, with solid brick walls, and one rock-hard, steel barred door. I kicked the door repeatedly, while screaming obscenities at whoever was listening. They wanted crazy, well they were going to get crazy. Detective Collins approached the cell and shook the door. "What the hell is going on here?" he said. "I'm trying to prove that maybe - by some miracle of a chance - that you are not guilty of murdering Natalie Boyer-"

I quickly interrupted. "So the body is Natalie's?"

"Yes," Detective Collins sighed, "I'm afraid so. I just found out a few hours ago."

"So, what now? Do I get to go home?"

"I'm afraid not."

"Why?" I asked.

"Because you are our prime suspect at the moment, and I have to say - it doesn't look good for you."

"What about Anna and Pete?" I said.

"They denied everything, and seem to be in a state of shock over the whole thing."

"They are lying," I said, "you have to believe me."

"I have made arrangements with Dr. Brandon to have you transferred to Sherbrook State hospital for a mental evaluation."

"Are you kidding me? I did nothing wrong."

"Calm down, kid, or it's only go to make things more difficult for you."

"What about my mom? Does she know about this?"

"Yes, a matter of fact, she signed the papers herself."

"You're a liar!" I shouted.

"We all want to see you get help, Justin. You seem like a good kid, but even good kids fall from grace sometimes. The hospital will be here to pick you up in the morning, meanwhile, I will have my officers get you a few blankets and something to eat. Is there anything else I could do for you?"

"Yeah, as a matter of fact there is," I said.

"What's that?"

"You can go to hell."

"Goodnight, Mr. Spencer," Detective Collins said, as he smiled and walked away.

I somehow managed to fall asleep on the paper-thin mattress, as the white lights illuminated above my bunk. At 6 a.m., I awoke to the sound of my cell door being unlocked, and two male nurses pushing a stretcher. "I don't need a stretcher," I said, as I adjusted my eyes to the light.

"It's for your safety and ours," the larger of the two nurses said. I wasn't about to argue with a guy who looked as though he could easily take a cannonball to the chest, and survive unscathed. Three cops overlooked the whole process, as the nurses strapped me to the gurney and restrained my hands.

The officers escorted them outside, where we were met by an ambulance, and another nurse. This nurse was the smallest one, and I could understand why they made him drive the ambulance, and not assist in the dangerous stuff. They loaded me into the back like a pizza being put into an oven, and away we went to crazy town.

We pulled up to an immense building that could have easily been mistaken for the living quarters of the Adams Family, or the Munsters. The place was a massive and impressive architectural structure, that looked as though it had been standing for well over a hundred years. The front entrance leading up to the driveway, was secured by a large barbed wired fence, and a guard station that was a checkpoint for anyone coming or going. There were dozens of windows, but not one allowed light in or out. The windows were painted black, and there were no people outside roaming the grounds or enjoying the garden that looked to be well kept. I started to get an eerie feeling about the place, and was in no hurry to get inside.

14. WELCOME TO MY NIGHTMARE

We were greeted at the front entrance by two female nurses, and Doctor Michael Brandon.

"Hello, Justin," Dr. Brandon said, "I am sure you weren't expecting to see me again, but what the hell—I am willing to let bygones be bygones, if you are." He grabbed hold of the stretcher and started rolling me through long halls and corridors that seemed to have no end. "It's funny how life works out—don't you think?"

"What's that supposed to mean?" I said.

"Oh, nothing, I just find it funny, that yesterday you were calling me some quack, and now, here you are, under my care. Do you feel differently now? Perhaps, after seeing how well respected I am by my colleagues, you will change your mind."

"No, I still think you're a quack, and a waste of space."

The gurney stopped hard in the middle of the hallway. "Now you listen to me—you are in my world now—do you understand that? I run this place with an iron fist, and you will respect me. I am telling you this for the last time. You can try me, Justin—go right ahead—but you won't win. I am a respected doctor of Psychiatry, and you are just some dumb kid who murdered an innocent girl and who has the audacity to blame it on Schizophrenia."

"What are you talking about? I didn't murder anyone, and I have no idea what schizophrenia even is."

The gurney moved faster now, as doors and offices flew by in blurry images. "Don't worry, Justin, we will have you back to normal before the jury can say: 'Guilty.' Because that's what you are, in case you are too stupid to figure it out."

"You are guilty, Mr. Spencer, and your judgement day is coming."

"Hey, who knows—maybe your lawyer will use the insanity plea, and you can spend the rest of your miserable life here with me."

"You can't do this," I said, tearing up, "I'm innocent."

Dr. Brandon disregarded me, and started whistling an old tune, as we stopped in front of the elevator. I watched as the arrow slowly crawled to first floor. The elevator rattled, and shook the gurney, as we ascended to the 7th floor.

"Welcome home, Mr. Spencer," Dr. Brandon said, as the doors

opened to reveal a madhouse.

"This is your new residence, and you will have plenty of friends here. A lot of them are just like you. They are here for various reasons. Take, Gilbert, here," Dr. Brandon said, as he grabbed the arm of a short, stocky kid with curly hair—who happened to be staring at a black dot on the wall. "This is Gilbert, and he likes to eat things that most people would find a little… let's say— distasteful. Gilbert happens to be quite good with a knife," the Dr. said, squeezing Gilbert's chubby cheeks.

"Apparently, Gilbert cut up his entire family with a fishing knife that his father had given him for Christmas. I guess after all that hard work of carving up his family like pigs—he managed to work up quite an appetite, and fried their remains in cooking oil, and ate until he was filled. He then fed the rest to the neighbors and their dogs, before running naked into the street and screaming incoherently."

Gilbert continued staring blankly at the black dot on the wall and showed no emotion as Dr. Brandon retold his story.

"Oh, you are going to have fun here, Justin," Dr. Brandon, said sinisterly.

My eyes looked helplessly at the patients, some of whom were talking to themselves, and others who appeared to be in a catatonic state. A woman with a jigsaw face stared me down, before laughing uncontrollably. Screaming and crying echoed from all directions, and the smell of urine and feces was overwhelming.

"Mr. Webber," Dr. Brandon said, "would you please escort Mr. Spencer here to Room 13. He is going to be our guest for a while."

You have got to be kidding me. Room 13? If this was a nightmare, I needed to wake up now. A tall man with a stone face approached and wheeled me away without saying a word.

"No!" I shouted. "You can't do this to me—I'm innocent." Suddenly, like some sort of demented chorus, my words echoed from several of the patients' mouths, "I'm Innocent, I'm innocent, I'm innocent—we are innocent."

They were all laughing and clapping as the orderly pushed me past them. I felt like a celebrity with all the patients grabbing at me. The orderly stripped me of my clothes and threw a hospital gown at my feet, which I quickly put on. He then pointed to the bed, where I sat without hesitation. The orderly then grabbed my head and pushed it down against the pillow, before proceeding to restrain my ankles and wrists with leather straps. I was left in the room for what seemed like several hours, just staring at the ceiling, and wondering how the hell I was going to get out of this.

I tried to close my eyes and sleep, but the noise was too intense for my ears. I started to scream as loudly as I could, "I want to go home———I want to go home!" Tears were pouring out of my eyes, and I desperately wanted to wipe them away, but my hands were tied, so I just let them drip down my cheeks. Suddenly, a boy peeked his head in at me and smiled before disappearing.

"Wait, don't go," I said. His head peeked in at me again, as he giggled and covered his face with his hands. "Please, don't leave. Come over here and talk to me," I pleaded.

He looked cautiously behind him, and then strolled in, with this constant smile on his face.

"What's your name?" he said, childlike. He was no child, but his demeanor was that of a young boy of no more than twelve.

"My name is Justin, what is your name?"

"Billy, my name is, Billy."

"That's a nice name," I said. His eyes wandered around the room like a child who was bored. He walked over to the nightstand that was bolted to the ground, and picked up the Bible that was placed on top. I noticed that one of his hands appeared to be disfigured, like it was put over a burning stove.

"It's Billy, my name is Billy: Billy the Kid." He pointed his finger like a gun and started firing, "POW, POW, POW," he said, while bouncing around the room.

"Hey, Billy," I said calmly, "would you like to play a game?"

"Billy likes games, but only when there is a prize. Do I get a prize?"

"Yes," I said, "you get the best prize, because you're a good boy, Billy."

"I want bubblegum!" he shouted. "Is the prize bubble gum?"

"Yeah, the prize is the biggest piece of bubblegum that you will ever set your eyes on."

He jumped up and down, while clapping his hands. "Oh boy, I want it—I want it now."

"Okay Billy, but first you have to play the game."

"But I want the bubblegum," he pouted.

"You have to play the game, Billy, to get the bubblegum." He looked at me in such a way, that I was almost convinced that he was a child, and not a teenager like myself. His face twisted in a sullen pout as he looked at me curiously.

"Okay, Billy, do you see these straps on my wrists?"

He nodded and rubbed his hands together in excitement.

"Okay, I need you to untie me, Billy— do you think you can do that?"

"Yep, Billy the Kid can do anything." He struggled with the strap restraining my right hand for a moment, before managing to release it. I quickly used my free hand to release the rest of the straps from my body.

"Ok, I win," Billy said, his voice cracking with excitement. "I want bubblegum, I want bubblegum, I want bubblegum."

"Ok, Billy, calm down," I said. "I had your gum, but someone stole it."

"Rats!" he said as he stomped his foot. "Who stole Billy's bubblegum?"

I briefly stuck my head out of the room and saw the orderly, Mr. Webber, standing by the nurses' station.

"See that big, goofy looking guy, Billy?"

"I see him," he said, "so what?"

"He stole your bubblegum—are you going to let him get away with it? What would Billy the Kid do to someone who stole his bubblegum?"

"Billy the kid would shoot him dead," he said.

"Then go get him, kid."

He ran out of the room, firing his imaginary pistols and shouting, "Where is my bubblegum?"

The orderly didn't even have time to react, as Billy jumped on his back and dug his nails into his big bald head. It was the first time I heard that big dumb son of a bitch scream, and it was pleasure to my ears. Billy had such a tight grip around his neck, that his face started to turn purple, and that's when I came up from the front, and kicked him in his groin so hard that I thought for sure my foot was broken.

He dropped immediately, as I reached for the keys dangling from his pocket. I noticed the one key was different than the others, and was marked *elevator*. I ran for it, as the orderly broke free from Billy's grip and gave chase. I put the key in and turned. The cables of the shaft started moving, as I continued to press the buttons in a futile effort to speed things up. The doors opened, as I pushed my way in and pressed the first-floor button. Two large orderlies come running towards the elevator, but I flipped them off before the door closed. I repeatedly pressed the button, as I stood there barefoot in my hospital gown, with my buttocks exposed.

The door opened, and I saw Dr. Brandon talking to one of the secretaries at the desk. I started running towards him like a defensive end going after the quarterback.

I saw blood, as he looked over at me with terror in his eyes. He attempted to move, but I was too quick. I tackled him so hard that he fell to the ground with such force that his glasses went flying and he was knocked unconscious. I noticed his car keys lying next to him, so I snatched them up. I scrambled to get to my feet, as I looked to see nurses coming from both directions. They had me cornered. One way was blocked by two females and one burly male, and the other had four males.

I took my chances with the female staff, and ran towards them while shouting, "Get out of my way!"

I ran through the two female nurses and they fell to the ground, but not before the male nurse had a chance to stick my buttocks with a needle. I burst through the exit doors, as sirens blared all around me. Panicked, I ran to where the staff's cars were packed, and walked up to the first luxury car I saw. A black *BMW* convertible with a personalized plate that read *DR.B.* I inserted Dr. Brandon's key into the door, and then the ignition. The engine revved, as I stepped heavily on the pedal. I sped up the driveway, and in one final attempt to keep me there, security closed the front gate.

I strapped on my seatbelt and drove right through, as pieces of wood broke off in every direction. The security guard ducked for cover, as I laughed while making an obscene gesture out the window. Thanks to my little friend, Billy the Kid, I wouldn't have to spend another minute in that place. I will have to remember to send him a pack of bubblegum from Canada—because that's where I was headed. About two minutes into the drive, I started to feel funny. My vision became blurry and doubled, as my coordination diminished with each passing moment. I could feel myself slipping away, as I struggled to keep my eyes open. The car swerved wildly between lanes, as my eyes became heavy. I was resisting sleep, but the medicine was too strong. A large truck blared his horn at me, and another shined his high beams, as I became dangerously close to crashing into them. I suddenly lost control and the car veered off the road, and down a deep embankment. The car missed tree after tree, as I saw bits and pieces of my life flash before me.

The car continued barreling down, as I almost felt a sense of relief, until I realized I was headed straight for a large pine. I put my hands in front of my face and braced myself for impact, as I drove head-on into the tree.

15. THE STING

I awoke several hours later in the hospital. I tried to stand up to leave, but my hands were shackled to the bed. A security guard watched me struggle from a nearby chair. "He's up!" he shouted to the nurse in the hallway. A pretty nurse came in to take my blood pressure and to ask how I was feeling.

"What happened?" I said, still disoriented."

"You were in a car accident," she said, "but you are going to be ok. You have a few minor cuts and bruises, but otherwise, very lucky. It was a good thing you were wearing a seatbelt, or it could've been a lot worse."

Detective Collins walked in and talked to the nurse for a moment, before pulling up a chair next to my bed. "You know you are in a lot of trouble, right?"

"Whatever," I said. "I shouldn't have been in that place to begin with."

"Dr. Brandon, and his staff are fine, in case you were wondering."

"I wasn't," I said dryly.

"Well, you better be, because if he presses charges, which looks pretty likely at this point—then you are going to be looking at some jail time."

"Give me a break," I said. "I'd rather spend twenty years in jail, if it meant not going back to that hospital."

"Have you ever been in jail?"

"No, I haven't."

"Then you can't say whether it's better or worse."

"I don't care. Dr. Brandon is the one that needs his head checked. If you could have heard the things he said to me. The guy is a narcissist prick."

"Well," the detective said smiling, "I have to hand it to you kid—you made one hell of an escape."

He was right, I did make one heck of an escape.

"I tried to help you, Justin, but you just kept resisting me, and now look at you."

"So, what's going to happen to me now?"

"Well, it doesn't look good for you, and I will leave it at that."

"Please, Detective… don't let me rot in that hospital. I didn't do anything, and I can prove it, but I need time."

"Time is something we don't have, Justin."

"Why not?"

"Because the media already got wind of the murder investigation, and Natalie's father wants you in jail. An arrest has to be made before the whole town loses their minds."

"You said a murder investigation, Detective... so she was murdered?"

"Yes, Justin, but you already knew that—didn't you?"

"And the cause of death?" I asked.

"A single shot to the head, by a semi-automatic pistol."

"Well, there's your proof," I said.

"How so?" he asked.

"My mother and I don't own any guns, I don't even own a *BB* gun."

"That doesn't prove anything," he said, "people buys guns off the black market all the time, and most of them are never recovered."

"But the death occurred just like I said, Detective."

"That only proves to me that you had knowledge of the crime."

"Please, Detective, give me a chance to prove I am not insane, and that I had nothing to do with this murder."

"Tell me, how exactly are you going to do that?"

"Allow me to wear a wire and go undercover. If I talk to Pete and Anna, I just know that they will confess."

"C'mon, give it a rest. Don't you think you put that family through enough grief? You can't go accusing people because you believe they are guilty."

"Please, Detective, I'm looking at a lifetime of prison here. You have to at least let me try and get some information."

Detective Collins looked at me curiously, and pulled a cigar out of his pocket. "I'm going outside to have a smoke, so don't go trying anymore of those Houdini escape tricks while I'm gone."

About 20 minutes later, Detective Collins returned, with a can of cola and the local paper. "Here," he said as he handed me the soda. "I got you this from the vending machine."

"Thanks, but my hands are tied at the moment."

He unlocked my right hand, and opened the newspaper to the cover story. It was a picture of Natalie, and a two-page story about her disappearance and murder. He hesitated for a moment, then started to speak. "I don't know why in the world I am doing this, but I am going to allow you to go undercover."

My eyes widened.

"You will be wearing a wire, and will be given two hours to get them to admit to their participation in the murder of Natalie Boyer."

I tried to give him a hug but quickly realized my hand was cuffed to the bed.

"Thank you, Detective, you won't regret this."

"Now listen to me," Collins said, as he pointed his finger at me, "there will be no funny business, and you get one chance at talking to them—so you better make it good. I don't know what it is, kid, but I want to believe you are telling me the truth. It's just that with all this talk of ghosts and stuff, you are not making it easy on me. Now let's see what we can do about getting you out of here."

Detective Collins pulled some strings, and before I knew it, I was back at the police station, and going over the sting operation. A few of the other cops stood around the table and listened, as we discussed the best strategy for handling this without coming off as suspicious. I explained to them that the big rivalry football game was this Friday night, and that Pete and Anna would be there on the field and on the sidelines. The plan was simple: I would watch the game, and afterwards, I would approach Anna and Pete with my condolences about Natalie. It would be during this time that I would try to get them to admit to any details about the crime, that only someone who was there might have known. It sounded easy enough as we were going over it—but I knew that nothing was ever as easy as it first appears.

"Okay, Justin," Detective Collins said, "your mother is outside waiting for you. I'm allowing you to go home, but you will be under your mother's supervision, and you will not be able to leave the house until Friday. You will go to school, as if it were any other day, and you will attend the football game later that evening. I will meet with you at the end of the school day to go over the plan once more, and to fill you in on any changes. Please don't make me regret this decision."

"I won't, Detective, my life depends on it."

Friday October 7th, 1988

Today was the day of the big game, and my first and last attempt at being a confidential informant for the Sherbrook Police Department. I had to prove those two were involved in the murder, or I was facing some serious time in a state-run facility. Mom hadn't said much to me over the last few days, and I had a suspicion that she believed I was involved in the murder of Natalie. It really broke my heart to think that she, of all people, would assume that I could be capable of murder. But I had no choice but to wait and see how this whole thing was going to play out.

The day started like any other day, with me riding my bike to school, and making small talk with Seth in homeroom. Everything was going smoothly, until lunch came around. It was pizza day in the cafeteria, which meant that everyone was in line for Grentan's specialty pizza (myself included). I made it to the front of the line, where I got my tray and then walked back to my table, where Seth was seated. I surveyed the crowd, looking for Anna or Pete, but didn't notice them sitting down until it was too late. While I was busy looking up, something had blocked my path through the aisle, and I fell face first onto the solid ground. I landed so hard, in fact, that it stunned me for a moment, before I realized what had happened. I look back to see Pete's leg sticking out, and Anna laughing hysterically. I staggered to my feet, still feeling bewildered from the impact of the hard surface against my head.

Trying my best to remain calm, I wiped the pizza from my jeans and got up to walk away, when I was stopped by Mr. Koval. "What is this mess?" he hissed. "What happened?"

I looked back for a moment, and the table had gotten quiet all of a sudden. "I fell," I said, "it was an accident."

Mr. Koval looked at me repulsed, like I was some worthless scum on the bottom of his shoe. "Clean up this mess, and try to be a little less clumsy next time."

"Yes sir," I said, "I'm terribly clumsy." I walked away to grab a handful of napkins from the lunch lady, and the snickering continued. I cleaned up the mess and left without eating anything. Depressed, I walked to the boys' room, where I stared at myself in the mirror for a moment, and tried to calm down. I wanted to be a snitch and tell Mr. Koval that those murderers tripped me, and that's why I was covered in pizza, but I knew I couldn't do that—not now anyway. I had to play my cards right if there was going to be any chance of proving my innocence.

It irked me to know that my life was in shambles, while they continued to go about their privileged lives like nothing was wrong. They showed no signs of being in mourning over the loss of Natalie. Of course they showed no emotion, they caused her death. The more I stood there staring at my own reflection in the mirror, the more infuriated I became. I was more determined than ever that those bastards were going to pay for their sins.

By the time the bell rang to signal the end of the school day, I was feeling exhausted. My mind was racing, and I had to meet up with Detective Collins to go over the plan. Seth had promised to meet me at the game, but I was not allowed to talk to anyone about what was about to go down. I rode my bike all the way to the precinct, because Mom was working late, and to be quite honest— I didn't want to be around her today. I needed to focus if I was going to get this thing done right. I arrived at the station, where Detective Collins was waiting with a small group of officers. "I am glad you made it, Justin," the Detective said. "I was afraid you wouldn't show."

"Why is that?" I asked.

"Well, when someone is looking at a hefty jail sentence, usually their first instinct is to run as far away as possible."

"Only guilty people run, Detective. I'm innocent, and tonight, I will prove it."

"Well, I hope you're right," he said, "for your sake and mine."

"So, what's the plan?" I asked.

"We are going to attach a wire to your chest before arriving at the game tonight." Detective Collins placed a small black box and microphone down on the table. "Myself, along with a few of the officers here, are going to be parked in various locations throughout the parking lot. This device will be transmitting your conversation to our remote location, and allow us to monitor exactly what is being said. I need you to speak clearly, and try not to have too much background noise going on when talking to Pete and Anna. If we are going to make this work, then we need a clear conversation between both parties.   "Do you understand all of this so far, Justin?"

"Yes, but what happens if they suspect me of wearing a wire and things turn violent?"

"The main thing to remember is to stay calm, and don't act nervously. You want to come off as sincere and trustworthy, so try not to jump right into a heavy conversation with them. You want to gain their trust first, and then go in for the jugular. If things do get out of hand, don't worry, because like I said, we will only be a few feet away. You scream for help, and we will come running. Do you think you are ready for this?"

I closed my eyes and took a deep breath before exhaling. "I better be ready, Detective, or I'm screwed."

"You and me both, kid—you and me both."

Everything was set for a final showdown with Pete and Anna. The wire was attached to my chest, and the cops were listening in to every sound, carefully tucked away in their vans, spread out in various locations. There was a lot riding on this night, and I wasn't about to disappoint Detective Collins with useless chitchat. It was a perfect night for a football game, with just enough chill in the October air to make you feel alive. I met Seth in the school parking lot before the game to grab a few hotdogs from the food stand.

"I didn't know you were a fan of football," Seth said, as he took a big bite of his hotdog, smothered in mustard.

"I'm not, I just want to show my support for the school. This is a big game for the Grentan Lumberjacks," I said, "and what kind of student would I be if I wasn't in the stands cheering them on."

"Yeah," Seth said, "but doesn't it bother you that Pete is the starting quarterback? I mean, let's face it, he hasn't exactly been a friend to you, in case you forgot."

"Pete is an ass, there is no denying that, but this is about the team, not him."

"Okay, man," Seth said. "Hey, I'm not complaining. I'm just grateful to be out of the house tonight. My mom is having her friends over for their weekly poker game tonight, and I would have been just sitting there as usual, as they exchange their viewpoints on how our generation is nothing more than spoiled delinquents and druggies. You saved me from all that, so, I thank you."

"No problem, Seth, thanks for coming. I would've hated being here alone with this huge crowd of people. I have trouble enough being around people I know—never mind a whole stadium of strangers."

"Well how are you coping then?" Seth asked.

"I stole one of my mother's valiums, because otherwise, I wouldn't have been able to deal with it." Dammit, I forgot that the microphone was on. I just hope the cops weren't paying attention to that little detail.

"Really? Wow, I thought there was something different about you."

"We better go find a seat," I said, "the game will be starting shortly."

We managed to find two empty seats at the very top of the bleachers. "Do you know anything about football?" Seth asked, as he pulled various junk food from his pockets.

"I know a little," I shouted over a screaming toddler that was seated in front of us.

"What do you know?"

"Well," I said, "there is an offense, and the quarterback throws the ball to his teammates, and then the defense tries to stop them from reaching the end zone."

"Wow," Seth said, "you really don't know anything, do you?" Seth chuckled, and stood up from his seat, while shouting, "Hey, if anyone needs a play by play of the game, then just ask this kid here!" He pointed to me as I grabbed his jacket and tried forcing him to sit down. "Justin Spencer everyone, world renown sports commentator—here with us this evening, all the way from Scranton, Pennsylvania."

A few people looked over and smiled, and then went back to eating their food and yelling at their children.

"Sit down you jackass," I said, as I tugged harder on his jacket.

"Calm down," Seth said, "I'm just having a little fun."

"Well the game is starting, so be quiet."

The wind started to pick up slightly and I pulled my hoodie over my head, while looking out into the crowd. I didn't see anyone who I recognized, but I didn't know many students anyway.

The loudspeaker turned on and the announcer welcomed The Lumberjacks, as they took the field. Pete led the way running in, as the rest of the team followed behind him. The crowd was crazy with excitement, and I could see a few supporters of the rival team getting candy and popcorn tossed at them.

I didn't see what the big deal was about a bunch of high school students throwing a ball around a field, but whatever. Anna was on the sidelines with the rest of her cheerleading squad, jumping ecstatically, while shaking their pompoms to the music blaring over the loudspeaker.

Pete was screaming and yelling at his teammates in the middle of the field, trying to get them ready for the biggest game of the year. I had my focus less on football and more on what I was going to say to get myself out of this mess.

I thought about a lot of things during the first two quarters, and none of them had to do with football. I wouldn't have even noticed that our team was losing, if Seth didn't scream every time they made a bad play.

"C'mon you stupid idiots!" Seth shouted. "I suck, and even I could have caught that pass."

I was trying to pay attention to what Seth was saying to me, but mostly, I just nodded; which he passed off as just a side effect of the valium.

Halftime started with the Lumberjacks down by twenty-one points, and their star running back injured on the sidelines. I needed the Lumberjacks to win, because if they didn't, Pete, was not going to be in a talkative mood.

"Halftime, man," Seth said, grabbing his empty wrappers from his seat, "let's go."

I sat there staring at the scoreboard, as I silently prayed to my father for guidance.

"Earth to Justin," Seth said, motioning his hand in front of my face.

"Sorry," I said as I got up from my seat.

"Boy," Seth said, "that pill really messed you up, huh?"
"Yeah, something like that."

"I have to go drain the lizard," Seth said, "do you need anything?"

"Yeah, I need you to never say those words to me again."

"What? It's true. Well, are you coming?"

"No," I said. "I'm going to stretch my legs a bit. I'll meet you back here in a few."

I carefully walked down the bleachers, and struggled to move through the crowd of spectators who all seemed to be headed in the same direction as I was. An elderly couple, who were walking hand in hand in front of me, slowed me down, as I failed miserably at maneuvering around them.

I heard someone behind me yell, "Move faster!" but the older couple couldn't hear them, or they just didn't care. I finally moved to the right, where I spotted an opening, and scurried towards the parking lot. I looked from side to side, and finally noticed a large white utility van parked out front.

I knew that the cops were watching, but I didn't know if they could hear me, so I said into my shirt, "Honk your horn if you're hearing everything clear."

Immediately, a red van, parked farther out in the middle of the lot, let out a booming sound that seemed to penetrate through the crowd. It eased my anxiety, knowing that I was not alone in all of this. I couldn't imagine trying to do this without someone watching my back.

I wasn't sure what Pete or Anna would do to me if they found out that I was working with the cops, but I'm sure it wouldn't have been good, considering what they did to poor Natalie. I walked back to my seat, where Seth was filling his face with junk food and sucking down bottles of cola.

"You know that stuff's going to kill you."

"Yeah, I know," he said with his mouth full, "but it's so good."

"Yeah, you're right," I said, as I reached into his bag and grabbed a handful of gummies.

"The third quarter is starting," Seth said, "do you want to leave after this? Because I don't see the Lumberjacks coming back from a 21-point deficit."

Seth continued, "Their number one scorer is injured, and Pete already threw two interceptions that-"

Before Seth could finish his sentence, Pete threw an interception right into the hands of the defense, leading to a pick six, his third of the night. The crowd started to boo and curse, as a few others headed for the exits. The coach ran onto the field screaming, and got right in Pete's face. I was seated back in the nose bleed section, but even from a distance, I could see the spit spewing out of the coach's mouth.

Pete kept his head down, but the coach continued to be belligerent. The refs attempted to calm the coach down, while giving Pete time to walk back to the sideline.

"See what I'm saying, man?" Seth said. "The team sucks tonight. I think I'm going to head home and try to get in on a game of poker with Mom. Besides, I'm getting cold."

"Okay," I said, "I will see you Monday then." At least I hoped to see him Monday, but as of right now, nothing was certain.

"Are you sure you don't want to join me?" Seth said. "I mean, it can't be any worse than watching this spectacle here."

"Nah, I'm good. I think I'm going to stick it out until the end; besides, I kind of enjoy watching Pete fail at something."

Seth laughed. "Yeah, he is a smug ass. Well, I'll see you later, man. "Here, you can have the rest of these." He tossed me a half-filled bag of gummy worms.

"Thanks for the cavities," I said, as he smiled and walked away.
Coach didn't allow Pete to re-enter the game and settled on the second-string quarterback instead. Obviously, Pete was not happy about that, and threw his helmet down onto the turf. He then started to run off the field where he headed for the locker room. Anna watched him leave and ran off to the locker room to join him. Things weren't going as smoothly as I had hoped they would. I needed to do something, and it had to be quick.

I whispered into my shirt, "Change of plans—they are headed for the locker-room—I'm going in."

The crowd had dwindled down to a few devoted parents, and a few fans of the rival team.

I had no problem getting to the locker room, where Pete and Anna were talking amongst themselves. I could hear Pete shouting in the distance, with Anna trying to calm him down. I felt like a spy in some covert operation, as I walked quietly and carefully towards the locker room door.

"It's okay, babe," Anna said, "it's only one game, and there is always next season."

"Are you crazy?" Pete said. "I threw three interceptions, and I cost the team the biggest game of the year—there is no coming back from that."

As I stood there with my ear pressed up against the door, I knew I had to make my move or I was going to chicken out. I suddenly lost my balance and fell against the door, and when it opened I landed flat on my bottom. Not the sort of entrance I was hoping to make, but at least I was in. Pete was sitting on the bench, while Anna stood rubbing his shoulders. They both snarled when they saw me.

"What the hell are you doing here?" Pete said, wrinkling his brow and tightening his fist.

"I just wanted to say," I began, my voice cracking with nervousness, "that Coach had no right to yell at you like that. The *Lumberjacks* wouldn't have won half the games they did, if not for your accuracy and arm strength."

"Are you being facetious," Pete said, "or are you really that stupid to think I need your support?" He got up and started to walk towards me, as I slowly walked backwards.

"No," I said, "I'm being serious, you don't get any credit. "You are always on the field giving one hundred percent, and the one day you're off—the whole town is looking to crucify you."

127

"I don't need your sympathy," Pete said, "so beat it, before I change my mind and kick your ass." His eyes were all that I needed to see to know that he meant business. I started to walk away when Anna grabbed my arm and stopped me.

"Wait a minute," Anna said, "I want to ask him a question. I heard it was you that pointed those cops to where Natalie was buried—is it true?"

I was starting to think that maybe I hadn't thought this through as well as I believed. Running out of there was not an option, because Pete was blocking the entrance, and screaming for help would do me no good because I still needed proof that I had nothing to do with Natalie's murder.

Pete walked up to me and punched me in my stomach. My face twisted in pain as I fell to the ground and let out a moan. If the cops could hear me, then why weren't they helping me right now?

"She asked you a question," Pete said, as he pressed his fist against my face. "So, did you, or didn't you, show the cops where Natalie was buried?"

"I--I had to," I said.

"Look at him stuttering." Pete laughed a sinister laugh as he put his arm around neck in a friendly manner. "Why you so nervous?" Pete said. "Did you see something that you shouldn't have seen?"

"I was just walking," I said.

"How did you know where my sister was buried?" Anna said.

"I think there is something he is not telling us about your sister's death," Pete said.

My heart was pulsing so fast, that I thought for sure, at any moment, I would collapse and die. My hands trembled and my legs shook like two broken stilts. I couldn't scream, and I couldn't move. I could only stand there while the two of them pressed me for answers. Pete thrust me against the wall as Anna grabbed the strings of my hoodie, and pulled until I started choking. I finally managed to scream out, "I saw you two. I saw you two, the night of Natalie's murder. I was walking in the woods when I saw you both with Natalie."

They both looked at one another, their jaws nearly hitting the concrete floor in disbelief.

"You saw what?" Pete demanded, as he pressed my face into the wall. With half my face being forced into concrete, and Anna choking me with the strings of my hoodie, I cried out, "I won't say anything!"

Pete eased his hand a bit, and pushed Anna away from me.

"What did you tell the cops?" Pete said.

"Nothing—I swear."

"The cops must've asked how you knew the body was buried there," Pete said.

"I told them I was exploring the woods, and came across the

playground, with Natalie's hand breaking through the surface."

"He is lying!" Anna shouted, as Pete held her back. "He told me, the first day that I saw him in the cafeteria, that he talked to Natalie, and he believed we were the same person."

Pete lunged at me, and grabbed a hold of my hood.

"What did you see?" Pete said. "And don't give me any more of your lies, or this will not end well for you. Do you understand?"

"Fine," I said, "I saw everything. Is that what you want to hear?

"I saw you and Anna chase Natalie into the woods and into the playground, where you already had a hole dug for her body. You gave Anna the gun and she fired the fatal shot."

I started to cry, as I was retelling the story that had been told to me, as if Natalie was speaking the words from my lips. Pete let go of my shirt, and I fell to my knees.

"What are we going to do, Pete?" Anna said.

"I don't know; I need to think." Pete grabbed his hair with both of his hands and cursed in frustration.

"Well think fast," Anna said, "because the game will be over soon, and then we are going to have a locker room of sore players to contend with."

"Maybe we should just let him go," Pete said, "he hasn't turned us in so far."

"Are you crazy?" Anna said. "He already took them to the body—it's only a matter of time before he caves and tells the cops that we were involved."

"I won't tell anyone," I sobbed, "I swear. I really don't want to die tonight."

"See?" Pete said. "He won't tell anyone. Besides, who is going to believe him anyway?"

"He can't live, Pete," Anna said, as she glowered at me. "Now be a man, and do something with him."

"What do you want me to do, Anna? I can't just knock him out, and drag his body outside in front of the whole town."

"God," Anna said, clearly aggravated, "you're such a pussy." Anna casually walked over to me, placing her hands around my neck, and squeezing, but not enough pressure to choke me—just enough to prove a point. She was letting me know that the cards were in her favor, and I felt it by the darkness in her eyes. "I killed my own sister," Anna said, "and she was blood, so don't think for a second that I won't come after you. If you even think about going to the cops—I will stop your beating heart with my own hands. Do you hear me?"

I stood there on the floor, like a helpless lamb surrounded by wolves, unable to speak, and trying to find any sign of goodness in those devilish eyes.

"Do you hear me?" Anna said, as she squeezed tighter around my neck.

"No, but I do," Detective Collins said, as he burst through the door with his entourage of police. Pete immediately started blaming Anna, while stepping away slowly from everyone. His face reminded me of a mouse caught in a trap, helpless, and nowhere to run.

16. HOMECOMING

"Get on the ground and put your hands behind your back," Detective Collins demanded of Pete.

"No," Pete said. "She killed her sister—she was the one who fired the shot. I was there as an innocent bystander. I didn't do anything. Please don't ruin my life, sir. I'm supposed to play ball at an Ivy League school."

"You'll be playing with balls, kid," Detective Collins said, "but it won't be in college."

"Screw you," Pete said, as he attempted to punch one of the officers in the face. They quickly tackled him as he attempted to make a dash towards the showers, and placed him under arrest. Anna just smiled slyly and requested an attorney, before she was led away in handcuffs.

Detective Collins held out his hand to me as I sat there on the floor. I reached for it and he pulled me to my feet.

"Was it true?" the detective asked. "Were you really just strolling through the woods, when you caught those two in the act?"

I thought about the question for a moment, and decided it was much more logical to tell a lie, than to tell the truth, which seemed like a lie anyway.

"Yeah, it's true."

"So, why didn't you just say that? Instead of fabricating up some crazy ghost story."

"I guess I was afraid of what they would do to me if they found out."

Detective Collins shook his head, took off his fedora, and scratched his scalp.

"Do you have any idea how lucky you are? I was going to charge you with homicide, kid, not to mention, committing you to the Psychiatric hospital."

"Speaking of hospitals," I said, "what's going to happen with Dr. Brandon? Do you think you could pull some strings down there at the precinct, and get the assault charges dismissed?"

Detective Collins pulled out a cigar and said, "Well, you did destroy the man's *BMW*, but I'll see what I can do. You did good here today, kid, but I'm still going to need you to testify in court—do you think you can do that?"

"Sure, after tonight, that shouldn't be a problem at all."

"Now unless you need a ride," the detective said, "I suggest you go home and get some sleep—you earned it." He lit up his cigar and started to walk out the door, as I called out to him.

"Detective?"

He took a drag and exhaled, "Yeah, kid? What is it?"

"I want to thank you," I said, "for putting faith in me, when everyone else seemed to be against me. You put your reputation on the line tonight, and well... it really means a lot to me."

Detective Collins smiled, and tipped his hat. "Don't mention it, kid—now go home."

By the time I walked to the parking lot, the whole place was chaotic. There were cops and flashing lights everywhere, and I could see several reporters already setting up shop next to the school. The coach, along with the entire football team, gathered around the police cruiser that held Pete, and demanded answers. The police escorted them away from the car, and I went in for a closer look. Pete just gave me this despondent stare that said, my life is over now. It was the look of a man that had been defeated.

I started to walk away, but noticed Anna pounding on the window in the cruiser next to Pete. She was screaming for her lawyer, and how her father was going to sue the entire police force for putting her through this. It was sad to know that she had no remorse for the sister she murdered, or the boyfriend who she manipulated into helping her achieve her devious plan.

I don't know why she murdered Natalie, I suppose the cops would find that out soon enough, but whatever her reasoning—it was not justified. It was getting late, and I needed to know what happened to Natalie, so I ran to the playground as fast as my feet would carry me.

I arrived to find a deserted crime scene, that was littered with police tape and tags, indicating something had happened there. The board that hung previously from the old oak tree, was now just a swinging rope, and debris and dead leaves that once concealed the playground's dirt surface, were now bagged and tagged at the precinct's evidence room. The place was quiet, and the cops who once scattered around the scene looking for evidence, were now on to the next case of burglary, arson, or whatever. I stood there thinking about Natalie, and how her life was cut short, and how it all felt surreal now, as I looked upon an empty spot of soil, that once covered her lifeless body.

The wind started to pick up, and the branches of the trees quivered above me. The chill in the air nipped my nose and ears.

It felt wintry, much colder than it should feel on an October night. I also felt something else in the air, something that, if I had to describe it, I would describe it as: a circle of comfort. I had never felt anything quite like it in my life, but it was powerful, and it was better than any high that a drug could deliver.

It was peace, in all its brilliance, and that's when I saw her from the corner of my eye. It was Natalie, and she looked just like any other girl, on just about any other night— except—I knew she was dead. She smiled, and seemed to gracefully glide over to me, as if the winds were guiding her way.

"What are you still doing here?" I said. "I thought for sure you would have reached your destination by now."

"I couldn't leave without thanking you. Besides, your father said that I had to stick around to give you a message."

"You talked to my father?"

"Yeah, and he wanted me to tell you a few things."

I stammered for a response, but I could do no more than stare at her mouth as she spoke about my father.

"He wanted you to know, that although you can't see him physically, it doesn't mean that he is not watching over you always. He loves you, and he needs you to look after your mom, because you're stronger than you realize."

Tears trickled down my face like a leaky faucet, as I took in every word, and every sentence.

"How come I can't see him now?" I asked.

"He has moved on," she said, "and once I move on—you won't be able to see me either."

"What's it like, Natalie? Is it scary?"

"No, there is no sorrow, pain, anger, or hate, only peace and serenity surrounding you at all times. There are no words to describe it, but don't worry, Justin—your father and I will be here to guide you towards the light when your time comes."

"I'll miss you, Natalie," I said, holding back tears, "and tell my father that I love him, and I'll be seeing him soon—but hopefully not that soon."

"He knows that, silly." She smiled. "I have to be going, I made them wait for me long enough."

"Who?" I asked.

"Everyone," she said, as she leaned in and kissed my forehead. "You'll see what I mean, someday."

She started to walk away and her body began to dissipate with each step until she was no longer there. I fell to my knees, sobbing uncontrollably. I couldn't tell if I was crying because I knew that I would never see Natalie again until I crossed the great beyond—or the realization that life was more unknown to me than I had ever imagined. I don't know exactly where Natalie went, but wherever she was—I knew that she had found her peace. It was not my time to find out what secrets death held, and to be honest—I was in no hurry to find out. I had obligations to take care of on this big spinning ball called earth, and the first thing I was going to do, was to patch things up with Mom.

Mom was in her room sleeping when I arrived home. I was screaming and hollering so loud that she came running down the stairs in a panic. "What are you doing?" she said, still drowsy. "Have you completely lost your mind?"

"No, I wanted you to know that the cops arrested Pete Tanelli and Anna Boyer, in the death of Natalie."

"Are you serious?" she said with a sigh of relief. "Thank goodness— are you okay?" She was hugging and kissing me so much that I couldn't even get a word in.

"I am so sorry for the way I treated you," she said. "Oh my God, and I had you sent to that hospital. "I'm so sorry, Justin—can you ever forgive me?"

"You don't need to be forgiven," I said, finally able to break away from her for a moment, "because I was never upset with you to begin with. I love you, Mom."

She looked at me, her eyes watering, and said, "I love you too. I have so many questions. Why did they kill her? And how did you know where the body was buried? And-"

"Calm down, Mom. It's a long story and it's late, so, unless you want to stay up for the rest of the night talking, then I suggest you wait until morning."

"Well I love a good bedtime story," she said with a silly smirk on her face.

"I guess I better put a pot of coffee on then," I said.

"Good, because I want to hear everything."

"Okay, where should I start?"

"How about the beginning," she said.

Diary Entry: #4 October 13th, 1988

The pages of my life have turned every tragedy into a somewhat, story book ending. Natalie has moved on to the afterlife, and her killers were behind bars, where they belonged— thanks to a little help from the Sherbrook Police. Speaking of police— Detective Collins, stopped by the house this morning, to wish me a happy birthday, and to return my diary to me.

I tried pressing him for information on the motive behind Natalie's killing, but he just said that "the investigation is ongoing," and that he would let me know if anything changes. I doubt he will.

I still don't know why I was chosen to help Natalie, or why she was murdered, but perhaps I will go back to see Amelia one day, and she can help me figure it all out.

On a different note, Mom and I have been getting along great, even though I lied to her about Natalie's ghost, when retelling her my story. I don't think the world is ready for my sixth sense, but I know the truth, and that was enough to help me sleep at night. So, until my next entry—Goodnight.

The End

ABOUT THE AUTHOR

Brian Joseph Rush is an American author of YA books. He was born on October 13, 1979 in Wilkes-Barre, Pennsylvania. He currently resides in Scranton, Pennsylvania. You can reach him through email at: boyrush33@gmail.com

Made in the USA
Las Vegas, NV
03 February 2022